BEFORE THE END,
AFTER THE BEGINNING

BEFORE THE END, AFTER THE BEGINNING

DAGOBERTO GILB

Grove Press
New York

"please, thank you" and "Willows Village" were first published in *Harper's*
"Uncle Rock" was first published in *The New Yorker*
"Why Kiki Was Late for Lunch" was first published in *The Threepenny Review*
"The Last Time I Saw Junior" was first published in *The Boston Review*

Published simultaneously in Canada
Printed in the United States of America

FIRST EDITION

ISBN-13: 978-0-8021-2000-7

Grove Press
an imprint of Grove/Atlantic, Inc.
841 Broadway
New York, NY 10003

Distributed by Publishers Group West

www.groveatlantic.com

11 12 13 14   10 9 8 7 6 5 4 3 2 1

morning, sun
then night, the moon
a wind blows, listen
open a window, a door
go on

CONTENTS

BEFORE THE END, AFTER THE BEGINNING

PLEASE, THANK YOU

at first, their people came and went. my children or the few close friends who worried about me dying, they came and stayed some too. im talking about staff people. nurses? not all of them. or they all werent schooled as nurses, years of classes, even if they act like they are or even do what nurses do. they do something every hour. if i try to say something, they start asking the same questions. what is your name? what is the date? where were you born? like that. or sometimes, como te llamas? que es la fecha de hoy? like im from mexico and just crossed, not american like them. im from here! ill bet my familys been here longer than yours! i was semper fi, cabron, and then i was an ironworker for ten years, were you? always, always has made me so mad, even if i dont say it out loud to these people here. i was cooperative the first few times, but then i just wanted to be given answers to what i was asking. like, am i going to get better? or worse? i didnt like them ignoring me, or acting as if what i said was not important. even if it wasnt. i knew what they were thinking. i was someone who didnt matter, who didnt count much. in the large, i know its true. i am a name, just another, one they think is foreign even, when there are so many hurting. but then, so what? i accept it always, in my life, but now too? it makes me mad.

so i started not answering, ignoring them back, or yelling at them. maybe yelling is what i was doing in my mind. maybe muttering under my breath is what i did. like, oh fuck off. what would yelling at them do for me? i practically couldnt move. so sometimes i did answer but lied, made up names and places. just said anything to shut down the questions.

every hour or few they would wake me up. i was dazed because i was messed up, but as much, i finally realized, because i didnt sleep enough. i wanted them to stop, and they kept coming at me in my haze. strangers with no names who just ignored what i tried to say who would say my name off a sheet. at night i became scared even, like my thoughts were exposed, like these people would be mad if anything wasnt exactly what they wanted. night that is early, early morning. nobody can really be feeling good to be awake, to be alive, then. not one of these workers. and i cant see their faces. i dont believe they look at mine. they dont care. i am weak, and everyone is bigger, stronger, tougher than me. they take blood or pull my body around. they turn on a light when it is supposed to be sleeptime dark. what does it matter what i think or feel? nobody sees this work they do, and i am just meat, a carcass. if i kick them with the one leg that can, will i at least be more wild tasting meat?

a few days like this i am so tired i can barely function. hard to think where i am and what happened to me. i dream but nothing familiar to my own history. one of them comes in and is telling me something. words as blurry as sight. i cant tell if it is kind or hostile but i am being shoved around, like i am doing something wrong, something bad. my body seems to be on something that i dont feel and i dont care but they care and act like i should too and they throw it on me. an arm with a hand, a third arm and hand, not from my body. no, it is mine. or was. i recognize it but it is inanimate, lifeless. i touch it with my other hand, pick it up. i was lying on my own arm. this hand. my hand and fingers. i know them. i knew them. im shocked. my own arm?

i am glad to be moving from intensive care. id say i counted the days but i dont know how many. my children are here to help me. i trust them. i wish they could stay, back me, protect me. its how it is now. i feel so small, and they are big, life-size, as big as them, unlike me. they are not weak. i dont trust these hospital people but i know i cant say too much. its hard to say much anyway. i dont want to say anything to my children either because they are doing so much already, and i dont want to worry them, or, worse, i am afraid they will think its me.

    you werent making sense, my daughter says. they couldnt understand you.

    i lied to them. they werent listening to me.

    daddy, im telling you, you werent making sense. you couldnt talk.

    it wasnt that, i say. besides, i know i made sense. i still have a brain.

    but your speech was bad, she says. its better now. sometimes you said things that nobody could follow. or you said things that were wrong.

    wrong?

    once you said you were born in new mexico. another time you said argentina.

    i lived in new mexico for a while.

    you said you were born there.

ive never been to argentina. i would never go there. a bunch of gringos. i said argentina?

one time they asked and you said you were born there. you said the year was 1994.

when did i say that?

when they asked.

maybe i got confused.

thats what i mean.

i hate argentina.

you said it.

i didnt want to answer their stupid questions. i started saying anything because i didnt care. thats why i gave a wrong name too.

it was that strange name, daddy. harry? ... i dont even know what last name you said now, but it was odd. we all wanted to laugh.

truth is, harry was a name i didnt know. ive never known a person with the name harry. harry anything. ive never met a harry, dont even know what kind of name it is, where a harry would come from. and i dont remember giving the dates or saying new mexico either. definitely not argentina. but it doesnt change anything. this is how they beat you down, and they make money. im meat to them, i know it. im nothing, im nobody. just nothing else is possible for me to do and im not going to do nothing. im not not saying something.

it isnt that i dont want to jump and hop around and be wide-eyed sparkly. if i could, i would dance for everyone. though i really didnt feel like any of it, even if i dont say so. i cant, much as i wont admit it out loud. any moving much is hard for me. i used to be strong. just the other day! just the other day, a couple of weeks ago. now, now these people come into my room. my room is more my bed. a modern bed that moves up and down with a control.

i cant find it, i say. i couldnt even buzz you.

she looked around the edges of the bed, under and in the sheet knotted around me. she found it under me, behind my right shoulder. had to leave a big impression in my skin, deep enough to cast a souvenir pewter model.

i couldnt even feel it? i say. how is that possible?

its okay, mr sanchez. you have it now.

her name is stephanie. shes mexican, mexican american. has that happy pocha kind of name. i remember the era, just the other day, when those educated lefties of ours named their children after aztec deities. my daughter we named gloria, my wifes choice. my son was joe, like my own dad and my suegro both.

but youre all good now, she says cheerfully. do you need anything? maybe youd like to take a shower?

i dont think i can stand up, i say. and with all this added weight, probably cant.

you probably havent gained weight, mr sanchez. and youre not fat.

i meant all the dirt on me, the layers of it with several coats of laying around sweat.

i could help you in the shower.

shes like sixty pounds and four foot tall. the other day i wouldve had to use binoculars to see her if i were on my two legs. from the bed, she almost seems full size.

i dont know.

i wouldnt look at you. id just stand there outside the curtain.

i meant i dont think you can handle me. your size, my size.

of course i can. i thought you were embarrassed.

embarrassed? hell, im proud when im naked.

mr sanchez, youre such a joker. i thought it was because im a girl.

normally id like it better because youre a girl. i dont feel too normal is all.

if you change your mind, she says, stephanie-like, sleepy and positive both.

its a good idea, this shower. and after i think about it, decide i will. but stephanie doesnt come back. now its scott, the other one who comes sometimes. there are quite a few of these employees. scott is the one who is confused like its three in the morning, not afternoon. he repeats things. for example, he says thank you even when it should be a tense there! or a relieved finally its done, or maybe he has to change the sheets, or dump the urine in the piss bottle, and always when hes leaving he cant believe he has this job and isnt still in the army.

he brings over the wheelchair. i roll and squirm and push myself to sit in it like its any chair to take a seat in. i land hard, as though the side that barely moves has petrified into heavy rock on the bottom and drags me down faster than i want.

thank you, says scott.

no problem, i say. the problem is standing up. the problem is not standing up. the problem is slipping off my clothes, even when its a tshirt and gym shorts. the problem is holding soap and washing when i bobble like im in a torrent of winds blowing into me from all cardinal directions. and im even sitting in a yellow plastic chair, a toilet seat throne. it is pounding to feel the water against me. it feels so good to get clean.

i cant reach the button that means enough. i talk. i cannot talk loud enough without screaming, which i wont.

i hear, is everything okay, mr sanchez?

i say i am done. i cant yell.

i hear, when youre ready, ill be there.

im ready, i say. hes not hearing me. finally i can turn off the water with my left hand. i just wait there, trying to figure a way to reach the help button. i try to lean and get it with my left hand, but it is a little behind me too. stand? try to stand? i lift off with my left leg and groan and there i am, standing! but i feel like a golf ball balanced on a plate. the tile wall isnt that close. not sure what to do, i begin careful movements. turn a little, turn a little, a little more, like a first time rock climber. i reach for the button and miss. the second shot is a hit though, i think, but no apparent buzz ring anything from the button. i push it again and again. im expert at punching it, could do it for many many minutes if i can stand much longer. i am there naked and wet, and i feel lost and pathetic because i cant do much besides this.

good shower, mr sanchez?

great shower, i say.

thank you.

he is drying me. it feels good. i am grateful.

i sit back into the safe wheelchair and he gets me a tshirt and clean pair of gym shorts. i dont want underwear, so i can pee quickly. he pushes me to my bed home. he pulls the sheet over me and it is comforting. i am clean. i am back to what i know. thank you, i say to scott.

least i know i can stand, i tell my son. next stop, up and down from the toilet. and then flushing by myself.

itll take some time, dad. you know that.

no rush. its all good exercise too.

were watching basketball playoffs. he likes them. i really like it that my son and daughter visit me and sit here.

whos winning? asks jannette. she doesnt even look up at the tv when she says that bursting in. shes come in to take my blood pressure and give me my evening cup of pills.

the girl across the hall, i say. shes got a no salary cap team. the girl across the hall, who cant be more than thirty, has so many visitors all the time i think they had to rent chairs. she had a stroke too, same every symptom as me.

shes popular, says jannette. she got lots of family.

my bp is still high.

whatre you doing in here, mr sanchez?

i think its the pills you people give me to keep my people down.

jannette laughs. we trying to keep you here cause you so pretty.

aside from the young one across the hall, how many victims arent mexican or black?

mr sanchez, you a nutcase.

see? im right, arent i? its an experiment being conducted.

you know you are a wrong man, mr sanchez, you always messing. but i am here for you, so you need something, you just buzz.

what i notice, i tell my son, is that all the help is black or brown until its like from two in the morning to six. those are the crazy people hours.

whatre you talking about? asks my son.

when they come in at three or four, and you can barely see them, its these deranged, sleep deprived white people out to get even. actually, those visits at those hours are harsh and blurry and 100 percent unfriendly. i dont know for sure what theyre for.

well, first of all, those sound like the worst jobs, so there goes your conspiracy. second, they must have something to do with your health. . . .

they wake me up so ill be tired all day like they are. either become like them or die from fear. this one guy just turns on a light when he comes in and starts talking like im the weird sleeping man in the dark. one night, reacting like a human, i cry out, whyd you turn on the light? he gets mad, you know, says its so he can see. now i know he turns on the brightest one to torment me and teach me whos boss. if i werent a cripple in bed helpless, id bust the fucker in his face.

i can ask about that, about you not getting to sleep.

youll probably piss them off more and theyll do more cruel shit to me. get to me when im finally having a sweet dream.

and third, says my son, i think over half to three fourths of the staff i myself see here is anglo. and the patients too.

and almost all of the therapists too, i say. my point therefore proven, that they rule the world, even if they dont have any players of importance on any playoff team.

pau gasol is on the lakers.

spaniards and argentineans dont count. and you notice how they dont even bother to learn to pronounce his name right? like its ga-salt, which they insist is not healthy, even though theyre the ones who soak everything in it, not ga-sun, which is the one and only source of all our light and energy! hes a star on the team too, not just kobe, whose name they did learn, as strange, and two syllables, as it is. always treating our heritage like its common and unimportant, even when its a pinche spaniard.

youd think speech therapyd be about speech. half my body went dead. that means half my face too. kristen, my therapist, taught me that even half my tongue went too. it is what i learned from her, its the most complex muscle in the body. thats why i sound drunk when i talk. however, we dont seem to ever deal enough with my speech or numb face.

kirsten, she corrects me again.

maybe its because of the stroke i cant get that right, i say.

nice try.

at least i got cover for my drinking.

i do think your focus might be affected.

i cant tell if shes teasing or not. she really takes her tests seriously. like there are answers in them. she has a library of three-ring binders she looks through until she finds tests for my homework, though sometimes i have to take one or two right there in her office. she times things i do. i hate this. i hate this speech therapy. i think shes making it up, doing some project on her own. wheres the speech part? i feel like its sunday school with mormons. i do not believe. im not a mormon.

excuse me? she says.

i didnt say anything. or mean to.

howd you know i was a mormon?

i didnt. maybe you told me.

no.

in truth, i had no idea. i was just thinking to myself and that sentence came out in public.

anyway, you need to put all the pills from the jars into the organizers.

all these? there must be a dozen jars of pills.

theyre all yours.

no wonder i cant talk right.

you have to be able to do this without getting confused.

what?

into each day. into the morning slot or afternoon or ...

i know what you meant.

and you have to look at what each pill requires. if its twice a day or morning only ...

yeah yeah okay.

you have to do it with your right hand.

but i can barely use it. i cant feel anything with it.

youll get used to it. we want you to do this when you get home.

they arent pills. theyre colored beads and and nuts and washers. i drop every one. then i dont drop every fifth one. i make it first try into the organizer slot only one in the five of the beads i do manage to get between my numbed fingers. not very good success odds.

i miss a lot, i say.

youll get better with practice. you have to be able to do this right.

so important that i am using my almost worthless right hand. i would never try to pick up real pills . . . but its good. it takes up time. i hate speech therapy and this will take me days of practice.

nancy insists on my being buckled up in my wheelchair to go to physical therapy. and she wont push me, unless were in a hurry. that is, unless she is. today shes in a hurry, and we have to go through an uphill hallway to the therapy room. i dont think shes a lesbian, though she has that short hair, ironed, tucked in shirt, fitted jeans, and never married to a man bark, and fire hydrant frame of . . . maybe its just her, who knows. shes nice to me, or means to be, when shes snapping. i like her like you do your hardass coach. even if i dont know her win-loss record.

    move your arm in. you want to lose those fingers?

    my right arm often hangs too limp and casual near the spoke wheels of the rolling chair.

    i tell you all the time. you want to learn when its too late?

    shes right. i pull my arm to my lap.

    now youve got it like you had a stroke and cant use it. put it on the armrest. it has to do what the other arm does.

    i obey and put it on the armrest. i understand her, shes right. when we get to the room, she makes me stand up with no hands. shes taught me and i try very soldierly to please her. i have to lean my body forward. apparently this is how i used to and everyone not in a wheechair does it all the time.

    almost have it, she says.

    almost?

    youre still favoring the other side. like its too weak.

i want to suggest that it is, really, kind of weak, but i dont want to sound weak or make her mad.

do it again, nancy says.

what?

stand up, then sit down.

now seated on the edge of a padded table, i muscle my way up, i sit down. like its an exercise, which it is for me now, not just standing and sitting. i do this until she tells me to rest. up, back down. i feel sweat everywhere, im hot, im out of breath.

you have to get more control, especially when you sit down. not just drop.

i meant to get them all.

the last ones were sloppy.

oh. sorry.

you got tired, she says.

im afraid of agreeing or disagreeing.

i do exercises on the padded table. stretches of the calves. then the quads. then i get on my stomach. i am supposed to lift my foot and calf ninety degrees, starting with the left. nothing, easy. when i try my right, its like nothing connects the two leg bones but kneecap. my calf flops on either side of my body. it doesnt hurt, theres no physical pain, but inside me, silently, it might be the worst indignity yet, so harsh i cant cry or rage. its as though i have been slugged very hard and the pain hasnt checked in.

this is nothing ever. i cant do it?

you have to work on it.

work on it? you dont work on moving your leg.

your hamstring. you have to.

i am on my stomach. i have no strength where i never even thought of strength. the plastic of the mat against my face, the pressing on it is how far ive fallen. how messed up this body is. my body. my life. my past is past, is back then when i didnt know, when i never gave a thought to . . . this. how is it possible i am this way?

you had a stroke.

i know but i cant believe i cant pull my stupid leg up.

you had a stroke.

its not time to quit yet. nancy wants me to walk. i stand to the aluminum walker and take one step, then another. i have to move my right leg right. bend it, pick up my toe. pick up my toe. dont hyperextend. she grabs my knee. now go on. go. pick up my toe and put it out in front and dont do this. thats good. thats good. dont go so far back. dont try to go so fast. step. step. step. not like that. stop that. dont hyperextend. better. better.

nancy buckles the seatbelt in my wheelchair because she thinks its unsafe to be unbuckled, even though i do it all the time. im too wiped out and whatever to talk. i am going to wheel myself in the chair because i dont want her to even if she is willing, which of course i am sure she isnt. i pretend to use my right hand to help push the wheel, like two sides of me are doing the job equally. i push as hard as i can but act like im not. i want to get to my room, and when i do, she says, see you tomorrow and i say the same, like i am looking forward to it and her.

1, patty speaks chinese. 2, the elevator operator plays tennis. 3, teresa does not speak french. and so on. this one, i tell my son and daughter, is easy too. but you see how it is. heres

another, which is worse, watch. i have to record the following
in a checkbook ledger. 1, ace insurance company, $90, march
17, 1981, no. 19. 2, deposit, $200.53 on april 20, 1981. and so
on, each a puzzle or test that is part of my speech therapy. least
this one you could say gets me practicing my writing with my
left hand. otherwise, i pretend i forget. if i say i forget, then i
guess it seems like i have more speech problems with addition.

just dont do them, my son says. im sure it cant matter.

i have to see her almost everyday. i did those pills so long
she thought something was wrong with that speech too. but
if you do these for for me, i wont look so bad, and my speech
will be much better too.

hello, says scott. hola. buenos noches? is that right?

its perfect.

just checking to see if everythings good.

too good.

good, thank you! just making sure.

alls good.

im finally leaving for the day.

you work some long hours, scott.

they never let me go. techs dont show, i get a double shift.

get some rest.

i wanted to tell you.

appreciate it.

thank you.

thank you, scott.

he is strange, my daughter says quietly as he leaves. very
odd character.

but you know, i say, i think hes harmless. hes here, doing
this.

are you okay, dad? asks my son. you almost sound soft.

i do need that other test done. you guys can do that for me? i really dont want to. my brain fries. not how she thinks, or why she thinks, but in the me that evolved long before the incident. apparently thats a speech problem.

i got it, daddy, says my daughter. its like that sudoku thats gotten so popular. only easier.

i could do it if I didn't hate to. i did them at first, a couple. just put it on some paper and ill write in the boxes.

she really checks on this like its homework?

you kidding? i swear shes going to detain me for an all-day speech camp for those of us with special speech trouble.

im not getting soft on the place or any of them. its like this typing though. which i hate. i hate the mistakes i have to fix, the waste of time, the enthusiasm they drain. you dont see them because of me. i make them right. im better at it too because im doing it, as you see. i type with my one hand. really its more one finger on the wrong hand. im right-handed, and now i can only use the left. im not bothering with the shift key or the apostrophe. i fix the other mistakes, slow as that is, many as there are. even by staring right down at the keys, i type y for t often, for instance, or o for p. i make extra letters where they dont belong, or i forget letters or spaces. i could make caps. not easy, bt i could. and apostropke.s. see those mistakes? im noy fixing them to show my point. that last little sentence has only one letter y instead of t typo in it. when i started typing, there was one in every word. sometimes now i put my right hand on this keyboard too, even though it really isnt close to helping. the index finger cant feel the keys. the right hand, and its fingers, have like a thick glove on it. the glove fits my hand so organically that it looks exactly like my hand used to. you cant tell them apart. im not getting soft. i am not wanting to scream and fight as much though, punish the keyboard the way i used to. i fix the mistakes as though im responsible for them. there are less of them to fix. i learn patience. i come back to the keyboard when im not so tired or just not so mad at all, any, every. i hate it, i know i do, that is the truth, but I get better at this.

im wiping the window clean with my right hand. its not really a window. its the wall in the ot room. im using a washcloth. its an exercise. i am upright for this. sometimes i sit and do something similar to this on an ironing board, where i also reach as high as i can.

    you think im going to get better?

    you already are, says deena.

    she, mostly, has been my occupational therapist for weeks. deena is korean. or her parents were. that is, all her grandparents were from there. she is always calm and slow-moving. i think it explains why she gains weight so easy. no metabolism. its what makes her seem like she knows more, has deeper insight, something like that. a buddha. i know its stupid. youd have to be here, youd have to meet her. even if she told me that her family has always been christian. pres-byterian, she frowns, which, she says, is so lame. but she says the word lame so profoundly and frowns with great, calm buddha wisdom.

    i guess i am. id definitely outrun a slug, crush him if i had to. i think. but i mean my hand. you think itll get better?

   i dont know. we never know. its hard to predict. brain
injuries . . .
   yeah, im always hearing that. i just want stats, not legal
promises.
   i dont know any.
   seems like nobody does.
   ive only been doing this for a few months.
   youre joking.
   no.
   but dont you . . .

my typing is interrupted by erlinda, the custodian. she washes
the floor in my room, dumps the wastebaskets, and cleans
the shared bathroom. for six years. shes from morelia and the
outskirts of mexico city last. she likes to talk to me because
the only other person she gets to talk spanish to all day is
the other janitor, beatriz, and thats only at lunch break. she
wants to know what i think. she was in walmart yesterday,
with her husband and two girls, who were excited because
it was the youngests birthday. they were in line to pay. they
were buying lots of things when she heard this woman in
the line behind them complain. about them speaking spanish. so, she says, she told that woman in english that it was
none of her business. that, see, she could talk in english.
the lady started yelling at her, threatening her, and so she
started yelling back at the woman. they just yelled because
erlindas husband held her back. then the guards came and
stood between.
   what was she yelling? i ask.
   i dont know. i was so mad. im not like that.

of course.

even now she is upset. was she wrong? it was her youngest daughters birthday, too, that was a lot of it.

i really dont know what to say. im okay with erlinda, but do i know what this other rude lady was talking about, really? erlinda is slow. thats not because she speaks spanish and is mexican. its because she is slow. not lazy. she is here at six every day, and the rooms are mopped and picked up. still, i wouldnt want to be behind her in a line, and not at walmart. erlinda is nice. but i dont know why she asks me. only because theres no one else, besides beatriz, to tell?

low-class people, i say. theyre everywhere, but especially at walmart. even though you save so much money there.

what could i do? she asks me. she has stopped swabbing the floor. shes not even resting with the mop as a prop to lean against. she holds it steady. what should she have done?

are you really asking me? do you really want me to answer?

yes, she says. please.

she says please. that makes it even harder. not because she is incapable of being so polite, but because she means it, wants my answer. if it were me, and i were her, with her family, which i dont even know about. please. sure, i sit in the wheelchair much of the time now. i go to the toilet with no help. i can sit and stand, hold myself to pee, clean myself. an hour ago i showered and didnt tell them. i felt like that was an accomplishment. like i was a big boy. i was proud and pleased with myself. she wants my opinion?

im not sure what else anyone would have done, i say.

she doesnt speak. she is listening, waiting for what i offer.

well, you know, i dont think . . . no. okay. youre a good person. i know youre an honest worker, just like you say. i know it. its not your fault where you were born, what language you speak. people like that woman, ignorance like that . . . you have to ignore those stupids. do your best, what you can, the best you can. what more is there? you cant help it if someone like that is in your line at walmart. wherever. stupid, mean people, theyre just that. theyre not most people. just like people who dont bathe. its not everybody, its not all the time.

thank you, mr sanchez.

you dont have to thank me. it shouldnt have happened.

my family was upset. i was. my husband is still.

mad, for you. of course.

we are so happy. we had such a nice day shopping.

beautiful.

i dont want my husband to think more about it. i am so sorry. i am never like that.

he cant help it.

but i didnt tell him what she said. i was crying.

well, okay.

he doesnt speak any english.

lots who do dont make any sense.

i shouldnt tell him?

you dont have to. tell him you just want to forget it.

thank you, mr sanchez.

please, no reason to say that.

its not the worst that has happened. im not sure why that made me so angry.

you were having a nice day.

exactly.

at walmart.

and my girls were so happy.

theyre still happy, im sure. theyll be proud of you. look what you do for them.

thank you, mr sanchez.

no, no. how old is your daughter now?

she turned three. the other is five.

so lucky.

see you tomorrow.

yes.

maybe make a special meal. tell your daughters you guys are having an extra birthday dinner.

she nods and smiles.

you just . . . move forward. why dwell on that ugliness? youre fine now.

ill see you tomorrow, mr sanchez.

i clear out in an hour. my daughter and my son are coming for me and i cant wait to see them and leave. im not good at goodbye, and not here either. im in the wheelchair i take home with me. it moves on its own. i didnt know how rickety my old one was. nobodys here to say goodbye to anyway, to thank, except stephanie. she works all the strangest, longest shifts.

i bet you cant wait to leave, she says.

i bet you cant wait to go home either.

i am so sleepy.

you do it all the time.

i only work these three days, but i have to sleep four days to recover.

shes still so little i feel like i have to hold the fired-up wheelchair so it doesnt accidentally take off and roll her down.

you need anything? she asks.

alls good.

see you tomorrow, she says.

yeah.

i like sleepy stephanie. ill miss her too.

i want to say thank you to all of them, even though theyd forget in sixty seconds. were all moving onward. tomorrow someone else here.

THE LAST TIME
I SAW JUNIOR

For years and years I hated him. I thought of ugly words instead of his name. I imagined what I'd like to do to him, and everything I imagined I'd do made blood. I mean red blood. I'd made blood happen in the past. Not gun blood, not bullets, not knife wounds. I wasn't a killer. But broken teeth, yes, absolutely. I imagined the bones of his nose being shifted to the side by my knuckles and saw blood running into and around his bleeding mouth. I imagined kicking the fucker in his fat gut once I dropped him too, a couple times bruising his ass as he was curling up like a pill bug, hiding the more precious, softer parts of his body. I never imagined kicking him in the face. I only wanted to fuck him up physically like he'd done me financially. We'd had one of those transactions that didn't turn out as good as he promised and which left me talking nice and making good to dudes from Juaritos, while he walked away expecting me to be as easy on him as his rich family were. I hated that nothing would keep him from owning up to it, because that was typical of him, too. He knew I was pissed and just how much and he knew why I'd never got back to him when he'd tried contacting me over those years.

Years and years. Lots of years that had almost erased the years of friendship before, when it was kicks. He had taught me shit back when we were friends, taken me where I wouldn't have looked and couldn't have gotten in. I hadn't forgotten that. He was such a *puto*, could mess so much up so easy, except he would do the same to himself. *Aquel pinche* Junior meant to do good, he just didn't always. I was old enough to have *chavalitos* in school and he was old enough for his to be out of it. But my bad life was past and my good life had me on a flight to Austin, a city I hadn't been back to since I'd left all those years earlier. And so one day I got over the hating. One morning I woke up and I didn't see blood anymore. Just like that.

I'd been put up in a suite in the hotel, and that night I'd opened the curtains to see the pink capitol below. I loved the view as if I'd made it myself. I opened a bottle of the complimentary wine, which, no expert, tasted nice to me. That's where I was—admiring the view, drinking the wine, when Junior showed up.

"How long's it been?" he said.

He seemed to have got taller and bigger, which made him taller and bigger than most men, but his paunch was paunchier, and his hair, combed maybe the day before, was getting gray, and his skin was chapped from too much drinking, and his teeth were yellowing. I saw them because he was so happy to see me.

"Years and years," I answered. "A long time." I dragged over another stuffed chair to face the view. He sat down as if the windows weren't there. Maybe I wanted him to admire the view like a girlfriend, a little envious. He just didn't care. "You want some of this wine?"

"What kind is it?"

"Free," I said.

"I meant was it red or white," he said.

"Freakin' Junior, you gotta be kidding." I poured the red wine.

"I don't like white wine," he explained.

"What, a bad childhood experience?" I said, regretting my meanness the second I said it. He was not looking rich. It's just that I'd never been put up in a hotel suite in Austin before. So I changed the subject before anything sank in. "How's your little brother these days?" His stepbrother, who I'd always been compared to positively, was already a state senator. Their dad had been a United States congressman forever.

Junior was a pro. Nothing startled him. "His head is so deep up it, he thinks the air he's sniffing is sweet."

Seeing Junior told me enough about him.

"So, look at you here in Austin! Looking badder than ever," he said.

"Things are the best ever for me," I admitted.

"Healthy, too."

"I get to the gym whenever I can."

"You still a Mexican?"

"I probably gotta carry them *papeles* for people like you, don't I?"

"You got papers?" He was laughing. "Do you?"

I was laughing.

"I use a pipe," he said.

I shook my head and we drank the wine and talked about his ex-wife I'd never even asked about before—a lawyer!—and a grown son who was living in Bolivia and our good days in Chuco, Los, Juárez, Burque, but never about what had happened, and we smoked until he was right, the view was no big deal.

"Let's get out of here," I said. "You hungry? I'm hungry."

Once we were out the hotel room door, I'd become the me of back then—both suspicious and feeling watched, even though we were the only people in the hallway, and far away from my old neighborhood. I hadn't had this reaction in so long. Back then it was Junior who cleared me in, and now, going down an elevator with him, being next to him made me think twice about whether I was holding, where I stashed it.

I could breathe outside. A part of the moon was up, the sky darker above it than below. It wasn't hot like it usually was in Austin, and it wasn't cold either. It was a night to be driving a convertible and loving Texas. "Damn!" I yelled. "This is lots better than I'd been expecting!"

We were heading to his wheels. "I was telling you I wanted you to come with me on an errand," he said. "You good with that?"

"Sure. Let's ride for a while."

"I need to pick up some money."

"You don't gotta worry about it," I said. "It's all on me, like I told you."

"I just wanna pick up this money while he's got it and expecting me."

His coupe wasn't close to new but it was worse than that. Trash had taken over the backseat area completely. And if it wasn't trash, it was well-disguised as it—fast-food bags and wrappers and cups, and beer cans, and a couple of broken mechanisms of some kind, in their gutted and skinned state, even clothes that, at first glance, seemed like shop rag material. And that was what I could identify.

"So what's up with you, man? You undercover, pretending to be homeless?" It was then I noticed that his T-shirt even had a hole in an unstylish place.

He didn't laugh. He ignored me. Or maybe his head was somewhere else. He still drove with a too-heavy foot, and even the car held on as he took it out of the parking lot and toward the highway. Both front windows were down, blowing around the shit pile behind us, but he didn't blink even when a sheet of paper exited and took flight. It was a car old enough to have wind wings, but only the one on my side had glass. It was open, maybe permanently, because it seemed as though it could not be adjusted. I was trying to move it because the wind was coming too hard at my face.

"Shit," I said to it.

"You break it, you pay for it," Junior said, almost yelling. "Air conditioning ain't cheap, even if it's only a Mexican AC unit."

I moved my face. "You are still a funny mother."

It was probably too windy for him to hear me say that. And so we didn't talk a lot but it was that good kind of not talking. We were on a dark country road, going I didn't even know where—east or west or north or south, but it was ranch and farmland, barbecue joints and taquerías and a Dairy Queen glowing brighter than any full moon. It was nighttime and beautiful stars twinkled.

"Look, so here's what it is," he said, slowing down to a coast. "This guy owes me and he hasn't been paying me any, and I want to get it from him."

"Whadaya saying, 'Get it from him'?" I knew.

"I sold him some ounces of crank." He waited for me to say something. "He paid me a little when I fronted him, and I been telling him he needs to pay up. I told him I was coming over to get it today."

"Junior, what the fuck."

"Come on, *hermano*."

"Don't be calling me that shit. I hate when you people throw in some Spanish."

"It'll just be a minute. I'll get at least a payment, you know?"

"Damn, man, I told you I'd buy you dinner, that it was on me. Not this."

He was slowing down, and then he made a left into a caliche driveway close to a bar named Gar's Bar. You could see it only when you were close enough, because the sign had no light illuminating its painted words. The bar's only light seemed to be coming from a couple of small neon beer signs in the window, Tecate and Bud Light. Other than that, it looked closed.

"It won't take but a minute or two. Just a minute." He stopped in the dirt lot and got out fast. I was sitting there, fuming. "Come on out." He turned back and leaned down at his open window to me. "Be hospitable to him, you know? Friendly. Have a beer." He was smiling at me. "Then we're outta here."

I was pissed off, but I got out if for no other reason than to move. I didn't believe it would take only a couple of minutes, and I didn't want a beer, but I finally followed him through the bar's screen door on the side. It was dark inside, the only light in the front provided by the beer neons. Already at a back door, Junior'd found a chain that lit a bulb in a hall. "Hey García!" he was yelling. "García!" Dogs got to barking, at least two big ones and a little yapping one.

"It's fuckin' closed," I told him when he clunked back. The wood flooring seemed to be the exact same material as the siding outside, with the same warped weathering. "Maybe even abandoned." The same brown outside was the brown inside, good for plants either way with a little water.

"No," he said. "I've been here when it's hopping."

Somebody came through the back door. It was an ugly dude wearing a blue jean shirt with dumb patches all over it, sleeves torn off. He looked surly until he recognized Junior. "I'll go tell Gar. You guys help yourself to a brew. They're right over there." He clomped out the way he'd come in and Junior got both of us bottles and opened them.

I didn't want one.

"You gotta take it. Take it!"

Shaking my head, I took it. "You know how stupid this is? I don't wanna be doing this shit anymore. It never even crossed my mind I ever would again."

He wasn't listening to me. He was ignoring me. Or his head was somewhere else. "Now look," he said. "I'll be doing the talking."

I drank at least half of the bottle. I was so mad there weren't any words. I started thinking about my babies, my wife. How I'd explain it to her if something went wrong. I wouldn't believe me if I were her either.

The sleeveless shirt came back, that screen door behind him slapping closed. He came in the big room with his eyes more on me this time. I was leaning hard against the pool

table. He switched on the light over it. I felt his eyes on me
while he and Junior talked to each other. I wasn't looking at
either of them. I took the second beer Junior brought me and
started drinking. I was thinking about it going bad. How we'd
be in the newspapers, on the front page. It'd be a good story,
especially because we were here in the state capital. Last time
Junior was popped, near Sierra Blanca, where there were no
newspapers, a bust that big would've been a few years of time
for anyone else. It wasn't meth, though. I hated meth too. I
hated people who made it, used it, were around it. And that
other was a younger Junior. This Junior now, well, nobody'd
have any sympathy, connects or not. And whatever it meant
for him, it'd be tough to impossible for me to explain my
being here, and sure to cost and damage me. I wanted to leave.

"Let's get the ball rolling," I said finally. "What's this wait?"

Junior was probably finishing his fourth beer. Dark as it
was, the white in his eyes highlighted the red veins. "Where's
García now?" he asked.

"I'm sure he's still in the house," said sleeveless. "He said
he'd be right out."

Junior brought me a new beer. I glared at him. "Let's
get this done," I said.

Junior went for another for himself and, nervous, circled
to the back door. "Hey, García! García!" The dogs barked
crazy. He came back toward the main room. "I'm going over
there," he said right in my eyes. "I'll be right in that house
right over there," he told me. "I'll speed things up." He went
out the back.

I was alone with sleeveless dude. I didn't want to talk and
I didn't want to talk to him. I could tell he was still watching

me. First I was rolling the cue ball against the cushions, then I picked up a stick and banked it around. Suddenly a pickup crackled along the driveway and parked in the lot and a couple of dudes came in. One wore a cap from a parts house, the other a welder's cap. They ordered beer. One took a stool, the other leaned by the bar, and the three of them conversed. I still couldn't believe anybody would think the place was open. I was trying to be a little patient. Then I didn't want to be anymore.

I took off out the side door and walked alongside the bar, making the dogs bark once I reached the back of the building. They were behind a short chain link fence, leaping and spinning. Their yard was next to a white house with a yellow back porch light on. It was probably where Junior had gone, but I wasn't sure. I turned and followed a dark but groomed path to the front door and I rang the door bell and waited. I rang it again and waited again in the dark. I rang it a third time, and then a fourth and then a fifth, with not nearly as much space between those. I had no intention of stopping, when an overhead light came on. The door opened.

It was Junior. Smiling. High.

"What's going on?" I asked.

"Just get in here," he said.

I followed him into a living room. There was a strangeness to it that took me some seconds to locate. It was that most everything in it was creamy white. The couch, the cushions on it, the lampshades, the legs of the glass-topped coffee table, the walls. But mostly it was the rug. A creamy white rug. And it was very clean, not a streak anywhere, as though it were still new, maybe vacuumed a couple of times a day, too. There was a little boy, six or seven, sprawled out on it, on his stomach, watching cartoons on the TV. He didn't even look up at me or Junior as we stepped around him toward the kitchen area. But stranger still was the man on the phone in the corner of the new creamy couch—except for a long-sleeved white shirt, he was all in black. He was wearing a black hat, a black vest, black pants, silver studs on the seam. He had a black mustache and goatee. Only his polished brown boots defied the color scheme. He didn't even look up as we'd stepped over what I figured was his son. His head was bent into the telephone.

We stopped in the kitchen by a glass dinner table, which was next to the living room. Below us was white tile. Junior opened the refrigerator. He brought me a beer. I wouldn't take it.

"What's the story?" I said. "I wanna get outta here."

As he plopped down, he nodded over at the dude on the phone. I already didn't like that man. But right then I didn't like anybody, and especially not Junior. "As soon as he gets off," he said. He put my beer close to me anyway and sipped his. "That's García."

"Gar?"

"Yeah," he said. "For short."

I shook my head. "What an asshole." I was mad.

Junior stopped smiling at this and he walked over to García, interrupting him, making García lower the phone. I couldn't hear what they were saying because of the TV. García stood up and they went on talking and the little boy paddled his feet and rolled some, happy with what was on. García looked at me. It was a little longer than a glance and he probably saw me shake my head. I was not interested in sitting patiently. I was pacing without moving my feet much. They talked close to each other's face and hands moved and García went into his wallet. Junior came back.

"Five minutes, five more minutes," he said. "Look, you want some of this?"

He actually seemed pleased with himself for getting an eight ball of coke, and he was unwrapping it like it was a real thoughtful gift.

"Are you fucking kidding me?" I wanted to scream and make a scene now but there was the little boy. I forced a whisper. "You fuckin' gotta know you've lost your brains!"

"It's not shit, it's not cut," he said.

"Junior," I said. "There's a little boy right there! Don't you even see that little boy right there?"

The little boy didn't look at us. The TV was there and we weren't.

"He doesn't see us," Junior explained.

I lost it, and I lost it completely. "NO!"

Everything changed. I probably was still screaming at Junior but I only saw him scrambling away as the glass of the table shattered after I slammed the thick bottom of the beer bottle through it and the shards scattered on the white tile. I didn't focus on what else was happening for a short space of time, and when I came back around the little boy was not in the room and García was hurrying to take his distant position at the corner by the phone and the TV was off. Suddenly Junior was there talking to him, both of them afraid to even look at me, their bodies squirming when they sensed I was too close once I started really pacing, hard, on the creamy white rug.

"We're leaving now, right?" I screamed. "No more! Now!"

Huddled, they were mumbling to each other, or so it seemed to my ears.

"I'm not waiting one more minute," I said. "It's now, I'm fucking DONE! You understand?" I headed to the front door but before I went out I turned. "You hear me, right? I am *so* fucking serious! I do not want to come back here!"

I left the door open behind me when I swung it open, the square light of the room projecting a path toward the parking lot. There were two more pickups now, and another car next to Junior's heap. I went over and thought I'd kick it, kick anything, when I saw that light go out as the door was closed. I told myself this was losing it but I had to—I had to go back there because it really did make me even madder that the door was shut. I kicked it hard. That door didn't open and instead pushed me back, making me almost fall, which infuriated me even more. I balanced myself and kicked, kicked, then really laid into it, and the wood from the jamb ripped away and the front door blew open. I saw them both standing where I'd left them. A quiet descended into me. I felt calmer. "Leave this open," I told them.

I don't know how long the sleeveless punk and a bunch of the others had been out of the bar, hovering by the side screen door. I was meditating, leaning against the coupe, looking up through branches of an oak tree at the stars—it was a pretty night on the outskirts of Austin, Texas—and it was only then that I saw them. I was feeling so much better that I didn't want to move yet, even though I'd finally figured what I didn't want to have to do next, which was to get Junior's car keys and get out of this place. I didn't uncross my arms when sleeveless took a long route to the front door. I watched him, and as he got halfway into the tunnel of doorlight, the big silhouette of Junior started coming through the other way.

He arrived smiling slyly.

I moved away from the coupe. "Can you drive? Maybe I better take it."

It was as though he didn't hear me. Pondering, he finally took a few steps back, into the line of light from the doorway, very close to a shiny new pickup. With his back to me, he fiddled with his pants until I heard the spigot splash of a urinating horse. As Junior arched his back a little, there even seemed to be a shadow of a horse's unit. It was ridiculous, and despite my renewed dislike for this man, I giggled when I heard one of Gar's patrons hollering about it—from a distance, not willing to approach.

Junior jumped into the front seat as if I were in the car already. I hurried in. It was almost like he was fishtailing in reverse, and the tires spit rocks and dirt, but neither the tail- nor headlights nudged anything and then we were on the road, windows still down.

"He came through," he yelled over the wind, "and I'm feeling lots better."

Maybe he expected me to say something, or maybe he didn't. Now we were driving and not talking and it was that bad kind of not talking. If I was a little drunk still, I didn't want to imagine what he was while he was pushing a speed impossible for me to check on. Not feeling like rolling up my window, keeping it and the wind-wing blast between us because I didn't want to feel as though I was sitting that close to him, I tried to keep my eyes skyward, at the stars above the staccato of ranch fences or crop lines. When I looked straight ahead, I tightened up with the thought of the force of a sudden mangling wreck. Looking upward I could make it more about space and time's slow passage, death peaceful and inevitable.

He had to slow down when we got nearer the city. Though I thought he might jerk to the left of the two-lane traffic going in, he only tailgated and changed lanes. But all of this slowed him down, and then we were back on the interstate, the pink capitol aglow on the skyline.

"Hungry?" he said.

I looked over at him even though I'd sworn I wouldn't until I got out of this car. He was smiling. It was his sincere kind of smile, too. "Let me buy. I want to." This was Junior grateful, generous.

"You remember where the hotel I'm staying is?"

"You don't want to eat? I couldn't have gotten it done without you, I know it."

"I'll get out at the hotel."

"Come on," Junior said. "Don't be that way."

A couple of turns and the hotel was a stoplight ahead.

"You scared the shit out of him," Junior said. "He didn't know what you were gonna do to him. Before you went outta control, I kept telling him you only wanted your end and I had to pay. After, I said I wanted it all to be done with it."

Green light.

"He had the money, too. Had it and wasn't giving it to me."

He stopped in the parking lot and he even turned to find a space.

"No, I'll just get out in the front," I said.

"Don't be this way," he said. "You were great! You were one scary Mexican."

I didn't slam the door, anything. I was so glad to be back in the hotel, hearing the live piano music. Elated when I first checked in, now I was self-conscious and embarrassed, and I crept over to the elevator doors, hoping nobody'd make me explain what I was doing there.

WILLOWS VILLAGE

I needed the favor because I wasn't doing well and I'd run out of places to stay and mostly money. I didn't really like it that my Aunt Maggy would know about my life, unless it was how great I was doing. I'm not sure where my embarrassment comes from, or if it's only a man thing. Could also be my mom and the years of gossip, and since my mom was my favorite mom, I always want to side with her no matter what. Maggy was an all-spoiled this and did-all-bad that but got away with everything because of her looks—men lined up to do whatever she whined for. Even now, she was supposed to be close to fifty, and she did not look fifty. I don't think many women look much better than her after thirty. Could be my mom didn't want to tell the truth about Maggy's age because, well, if my mom wasn't as pretty, she was probably a better cook. Maybe Maggy was a lot younger. It was possible, if you ask me. I was here looking at her.

I wouldn't have recognized her if I weren't at her kitchen table. Last time I saw her I was at most fifteen. She'd visited our house in El Paso a few times but you know how that is. I didn't stick around for the family things once I was older, and even when I kissed her hello and good bye, I didn't see or hear her. I was a teenager then. Now I was a man with a wife and a baby and another one coming, too. I was a man, and I realized my aunt was a woman who, well, was hard not to look at.

"I'm trying for everything," I told her. "I only want a job that I can count on." I'd told her about the three I'd already had. Two were in construction, which I didn't really want and didn't last more than a week, and the last, in a restaurant, which I only took to have anything, but it went from early morning to early evening, and I couldn't look for one better.

"You listen to Jim's advice when he gets back, Guillermo. He won't be away that long." Jim was her husband. He was in Chicago and on his way to Brazil and he'd be gone for a couple or even a few weeks. I didn't ask her what he did. He had a last name that I couldn't pronounce. My mom would get mad at my dad for saying this, but he would call him a rich *gabacho* son of a Zabludovsky—that *chilango* newscaster—living it up inside Mexico. My mom didn't like him making sexual remarks about Maggy, even if everybody did. I think Maggy'd had at least two other last names since she'd been married at least two other times. Her family name was Santamaria, which also made my father wink sarcastically.

"Billy," I told her. "Everybody always calls me Billy."

"Guillermo is much better," she insisted. "It's more mature, and it's a manly name." The jewelry on her arms and ears tingled like in a breeze that also swayed her long black hair.

I preferred Billy. I didn't like to be formal. I didn't want to sound like I just crossed. I liked people to know I was American, born and raised. I had an uncle who was more tattooed cholo, who called himself Memo, and I didn't want that. Besides, wasn't she a Maggy? A grateful guest, I didn't say more.

She was drinking wine. It was from a big jug, not that there weren't plenty of those other kind you usually saw in restaurants—a rack of them and some more sitting on the table and counter. I'd already said no thank you. I didn't really know how to drink wine. It wasn't just the wine, but the entire kitchen was loaded up like a mall gourmet store. She had the complete set of copper pots and pans, and a lot that weren't copper, hanging from above the stove, she had another rack of wineglasses, and she had so many utensils that it was more like a tool shop to me. There were appliances, too. Not one blender but two. A food processor and an industrial toaster. A bread maker. A pasta machine. New, new, new. She had knives in several wooden blocks, towels, and the counters were weighted with so many plastic and glass bottles of this and that that you wondered what could be in the cabinets. On the space above them, Mexican pottery, Mexican dishware. On the table where I was sitting, a floral bouquet, a setting. It was beautiful and it looked real but it wasn't—I smelled them and she told me. On the table and on the floor near it, a pile of unread beauty magazines, half in Spanish, a couple that were the same, but one was American and the other from Mexico—or Spain, or wherever, I didn't know.

"A beer then?"

"Sure."

She opened a side of the silver refrigerator. It seemed like things would fall out it was so stuffed. She dug around— I felt like I should get up and help her take stuff and hold things—until she found a green bottle and somehow seemed to know right where an opener was. She gave it to me and I probably shouldn't have stared at it first and then so long. It had foil around its top and I don't think I could read the language it was in.

"Jim loves it, thinks it's the best."

I stopped what I was doing and drank. It had a strange taste to me. "Wow, yeah, really good. Thank you."

"I have to tell you about Lorena."

I nodded and I sipped the strange beer.

"She's been staying here, too. Downstairs. It's where I'd have you stay if she wasn't here already. She's been having trouble. We're very good friends."

"Sure," I said. "I'm really thankful for your help."

"We're family. You're my sister's son, so you're my son, too."

I had a room up the carpeted stairs. It was a girl's room, teenager, or like that. It was confusing-looking. She said it was her play room and she was sorry it was a mess. I told her to not be sorry, that I didn't care. I didn't either, even though it was a girl's room. There were two big containers of little boxes of dolls—not all in their store boxes—and a few facedown and sideways on shelves, and knitting boxes and an antique sewing machine and makeup jars and compacts and brushes and lipsticks—all in shoeboxes piled and stacked—and photos everywhere, all in more shoeboxes but also in a pile on the floor. It was hard to know where to put my suitcase except in the middle of the room. And the walls were wallpapered. That was more old-ladyish to me, a pink color, with red velvet roses. The kind of bed had a name that meant it wasn't just the bed. It was also considered a couch, she told me. To me it was a bed and only a bed and it had lots of pillows, girl pillows, and a frilly cover. It was fine. I was happy. I needed a place to sleep. And the TV on the floor—like it didn't work and wasn't really supposed to be in there—it worked. I think there was another bedroom next to this one, but that door was closed and I didn't look. There was a bathroom and then there were double doors, right across from where I was, that opened to the master bedroom. One of those doors was open. It was a huge room, as beautiful as any hotel, a king-size bed that didn't even take up too much space. There was still plenty between it and all the dressers and mirrors. It was a lot better than a hotel.

I was up in the morning, early. I decided to dress as nice as I could. I wore a white shirt and put on a tie. I didn't have a sports coat. Besides, though it wasn't hot, it wasn't cold enough. And I didn't own one. Aunt Maggy's was in a tract development and it was called Willows Village. I don't know why I thought about it so much even before I drove in, when it was only part of the directions. I did. And then the actual image of the sign on the block wall entrance to the village practically burned my eyes. It was trapped in my head and when I would think of Aunt Maggy, I'd see a droopy green tree and those words. Her house was right next to the freeway, which was a good thing if you were driving to work and had to get on the freeway, which maybe most everybody else did. We had highways in El Paso but nothing like this one right next to the village. Even in the morning, or maybe especially, it was loud. I couldn't really believe how loud it was. It almost made me stop. But there was nothing to look at, to see. The freeway was just above and on the other side of the houses across the street. You couldn't see the cars or trucks or motorcycles. Their sounds, though, they made, like, shadows my eyes wanted to see but couldn't. So I got in and rolled down the windows and joined the noise, too, the looking-for-the-job driving noise, and I drove past the Willows Village sign and into the job world.

There were lots of jobs in Santa Ana and around it when you looked in the paper. There were lots of construction sites, but I saw so many car dealerships that I finally decided, I really made made up my mind. I wanted to be a car salesman. I had a high school friend from El Paso, up a couple of streets and right near Fort Boulevard, who told me that when he moved out here, that he started at car sales and the next thing he knew, he was making a really great living and he loved it. I tried to find his new address before I left El Paso. He'd grown up with his grandma, and when I went over, she didn't live there. The people who did said they bought the house after she died, and they had no idea where he was. I just thought what he did was original and smart. Not that it was. Everybody had heard of car salesmen. What was original was to be one. And after the other jobs, it was even more original. So I started stopping at dealers on Harbor Boulevard and I went right in, shaking hands, saying I was looking for a job as a car salesman. I filled out applications, and I talked to a couple of managers, too. I think that I spoke Spanish was a definite asset. Definitely at two places. One used, one new. The new car dealer manager asked if I had a coat, a couple, even. I said I did. I think he didn't like my white shirt or my tie—something in his eyes—so I decided that if he called back, I'd get something. I'd borrow the money. I thought I had a really good shot.

I wasn't sure if I should get back to Aunt Maggy's so early in the afternoon or not. I wasn't sure if she would like it if I didn't, say, look for a job until the evening. I also didn't know where else to go besides there. When I stayed with an old friend and his wife for a couple of weeks, those days I didn't work, they were working. I could watch TV. I didn't know if Maggy had a routine or not. I had a key but the door was a little open. I mean, it wasn't closed. Still, I rang the doorbell.

"Hello!" Aunt Maggy yelled.

I went ahead and pushed the door open.

"What are you doing ringing the bell? Just come in! You live here!"

I kind of nodded and muttered a thanks, okay. They were at the table and it was that jug of wine. Maybe even another one just like it. It was hard to see them, though. There was a big glass window behind them, and the sun was out. I was afraid I would be looking funny at them as I got to the table.

"How'd it go?" Aunt Maggy asked. She was wearing a one-piece bathing suit. She was a *chichona* woman and it was hard not to know that, especially when she was wearing a bathing suit. I still saw the Willows Village sign, which I'd just passed again, in my head, too. It didn't feel right.

"Pretty good," I said. "I really think I'm gonna get one."

"*¡Qué bueno!*" said Aunt Maggy.

"One doing what?" the other woman said. I knew it was Lorena.

"Oh," my Aunt Maggy said, "this is Lorena."

I shook her hand. "I'm Billy," I said.

"Guillermo," Aunt Maggy said.

"Doing what?" Lorena said.

Aunt Maggy started laughing. "I didn't even ask what." She laughed and so did Lorena. They thought it was funny, and they each took another drink and giggled.

"Do you want some wine?" Lorena asked. Beside on a rack, there were a few clean wineglasses on the counter near the kitchen table and she reached over and got one and poured me a glass.

"He doesn't drink wine," Aunt Maggy told her.

"I'm sorry," Lorena said.

"I can." That made her feel better. I sipped some. I didn't really like wine, I guess.

"So, tell us," Lorena said. "What kind of job?"

"Car salesman."

I think they wanted to laugh. Maybe. Except they didn't.

"Is that what you want?" Lorena asked.

"I think you can make good money at it." I almost was going to tell her about my friend in El Paso. I didn't really like the wine, but I drank some more.

"Good for you," Aunt Maggy said. "I think they'll be lucky to get you."

We clinked the wineglasses. We all took drinks for a toast and Maggy refilled Lorena's, then hers.

"I bet you're hungry," Maggy said to me.

"I'm hungry," said Lorena. "What can we make?"

"There's so much," she said.

There was, too. The kitchen was so full of everything.

"Let's just get takeout. Chinese? Italian? How about subs?"

"Yum," said Lorena.

We were all supposed to pick, until Aunt Maggy said she'd get three kinds and we'd share. She got on the phone and she was ordering.

"What about you?" I asked Lorena. "What do you do?"

She didn't answer quickly. "I fight for a woman's rights. I fight against dirty husbands."

Maggy, still on the phone, made eyes at her and shook her head.

I decided not to ask.

Lorena was in a bathing suit, too, but she had a towel bathrobe over her. Hers was a two-piece, a bikini, because once in a while it opened. It was a good bet that all of her figure was good, too. She had an accent. I couldn't figure it out. It might have been Mexican, but if she spoke Spanish, then they would be speaking Spanish. Her eyes were hazel but also green. Maybe her shoulder-length hair was dyed. It was brown with yellow in it. I thought her hair should be dark brown. She was my age, give or take a few years.

Off the phone, Aunt Maggy took another gulp of wine and got up and then so did Lorena. Too much to look at, so I looked down and out the window to the big backyard. I listened as Maggy took out plates from a cabinet and brought them to the table. Lorena went to the sink and came back with a dishrag and wiped the table. Both of them brushed up against me when they came back. It was that I was in a chair that was in the way, the one I sat in without thinking when I walked in. I considered moving.

"Would you rather have beer with your sandwich?" Lorena asked me. "If you really don't like wine."

I decided I had to look up when I answered and she was very close to me, her robe loosely closed, and she was standing, and I was sitting. It was hard to keep my eyes steady. "Well," I said, ". . . no I think I should stay with the wine." I finished my first glass and then she leaned across me and got the bottle and filled it back up. The jug was almost empty, so then she put the last of the wine in hers. She was warm.

"Open another if you want," Maggy said. "Open this one." She handed Lorena a smaller bottle and she looked around for the wine opener. Lorena handed it and the bottle to me.

The truth is, I wasn't sure how it worked. It had the curled screw but also something else. I don't know if they watched me, but I pulled the cork out the only way I knew. "So you guys went to, like, the beach?" I asked. I left the bottle on the table because all of the glasses were full.

"My neighbor Paula has a pool," said Maggy. "You want to go swimming? I'm watching it for her while they're away."

"It's delicious!" said Lorena. "It's so nice over there. You have to go."

Ready for the food to arrive, Aunt Maggy started cleaning the kitchen. "I don't know how I get such a mess all the time," she said.

Lorena sat down again, looked over at me, drank wine, and sighed. "Are you as hungry as I am?" she asked me.

I was trying to be quick to answer.

"Don't be so shy," she said. "Just say yes."

"Okay," I mumbled.

"Yes yes yes," said Maggy near the sink. "We say yes!"

"Yes!" said Lorena more loud. They laughed. Then

Lorena got up from her chair and put her arms around me and hugged me. "Please don't mind us drunk women."

"What did she say?" Aunt Maggy asked over there.

"I told him not to mind us drunk girls."

"Mind us? What man is going to mind drinking with us? Right, Guillermo? You better say yes!"

They laughed staring at me. I made myself laugh along with them, but I wasn't sure what else to do. I was doing more than sitting there but it couldn't look like much. I drank more wine and was feeling it, not noticing the taste so much. I was thinking of how warm Lorena was when she hugged me and I still felt her breasts pressing on me, too, stuck to me like that sign was.

The doorbell rang. As I turned back to look, Aunt Maggy yelled, "Hello!" It was a young delivery guy and he was holding a white bag. The door was wide open, not because he opened it but because it was wide open. I guess I forgot to shut it.

Maggy came around the corner from the kitchen. "Come on in!" she told him. She was in the kitchen and then went through another door. "I can't find my purse!" she yelled.

He stopped near the table. Lorena took the bag from him and was pulling submarine sandwiches out. Lorena's robe wasn't even tied anymore. I was standing for a minute and then I sat, but I moved my chair, making more room to pass. The guy didn't talk. He was staring, blank. I wondered what he was thinking about them in their bathing suits. Maybe he was more used to it than me.

Suddenly Lorena yelled. "It's over here, Maggy!" She held the purse, which had been in the corner.

"I am so dingy," Aunt Maggy said when she came back in the kitchen. When she opened the purse, it exploded money like a jack-in-the-box. Bills popped out everywhere, a fountain of crumpled greenbacks. Maggy made a loud sigh and an "*¡Ay, Dios!*" and rolled her eyes, like it was the fault of the purse. Lorena picked up the cash and I helped, too, and when Aunt Maggy started counting out a few—"How much?" she asked the delivery guy—I was already making a neat stack of mine. I was going to do the same thing with what Lorena piled on the table but I didn't. They were of all kinds of denominations and I thought they could be sorted, too, but I didn't do that, either. When the guy left, Aunt Maggy stuffed them right back without a second thought and clicked the purse closed.

I knew I was going to get one of those jobs. I mean, I applied at more dealers, too, but my gut feeling told me that it was going to happen with those first ones interested in me. I was trying to figure out which would be better money, used cars or new car sales. I didn't have enough information about either, so I just thought about it. One strong guess was that the new car job would require better clothes. Maybe a suit, but at least a couple of good coats and pants, and for both, some dress shirts. Ties, too. I felt it even more when I dropped in on them again telling them I was still looking, still hungry for this work. I think they both liked me, but I also felt like they might have seen that I was wearing the same white shirt and tie. I could not go there again in the same shirt and tie, and if they did call, I had to have something else, no matter what. So I stopped at a store afterward and bought another of each. They weren't the most expensive, but I was almost out of money, and that wasn't good. I needed to buy a few shirts. And the rest. I could get some money from home, from my parents. My wife, Suzie, was living with my *suegros*, her parents, so we wouldn't have to be spending on rent.

This time I got in late. I took a long drive once it got to be afternoon, got stuck in a lot of freeway traffic I didn't know how to get out of, and I had to go to a few stores to find the shirt and tie once I found a mall. I had to put gas in my car, too. I went to a drive-through and got a large soda and stayed parked in the lot a while. It made me feel bad that I would have to borrow from my parents again. My mom, anyway. She wouldn't even tell my dad. It was nice sitting. I needed it. I even turned off the radio. I think I was there a long time. I thought of going to a bar, but it didn't seem right to buy beer, too. And there was plenty of beer and wine at Aunt Maggy's. I missed home and wished this would stop. It was getting dark. The automatic lights were already on the Willows Village sign when I drove in.

"Did you get a job?" Aunt Maggy asked.

"No, not yet."

"You're so late. I thought maybe you found one."

Lorena came to the kitchen from her room. She looked concerned, too.

"Are you hungry?" Maggy asked.

"What'd you buy?" asked Lorena, interrupting. I had the shopping bag in my hand. "Let me see," she said, reaching for it.

"It's just a shirt and tie."

She already knew it because she took them out before I answered. I don't think she thought much of them.

"You have to be hungry. Sit with me." Aunt Maggy sat down at the kitchen table. It was full of all kinds of stuff, not only the wine bottles and glasses, but a stack of folded towels and women's colorful underwear, top and bottom. Even a full grocery bag not unloaded. "Lorena, can you serve him that Chinese food? I think there's a lot."

"I can do that," Lorena said. "Of course." She kind of stepped into the kitchen like it was too dark to see, even though the bright panels of ceiling lights were on. "Where is it?" There was so much everywhere.

"It's there. Somewhere. Maybe I put it in the fridge. I don't remember now."

Lorena opened the refrigerator door and stared, then she stuck her hand in like touching any one thing wrong might tip over something else. "Way in the back somehow," she announced. "But it is here."

"Are you okay? *¿Todo bien*, Guillermo?"

I guess I was grouchy. For one, I felt like being called Billy. "I think I'm a little tired is all. I'm fine."

Lorena was trying to get to the microwave. She had to move lots of things.

"You have to put it on a plate," said Maggy. "Those take-out boxes have wire."

"I already know. I already have it on a plate."

Maggy stared at the mess on the table like it was some-one's fault. "Do you need your clothes washed?"

"I was going to ask. I sure do."

She picked up the tie I just bought. It was on the table, too. "Do you need some ties? Jim has so many ties. I think he has some shirts that would fit you, too."

I couldn't believe it! "That would be so great, Tía," I told her.

To make room on the table, Aunt Maggy had Lorena take the towels and underwear and my two things upstairs. I really liked the Chinese food. It was the best I'd ever eaten.

When I woke up I couldn't think of what else to do really. I had gone to every new and used car dealer in Santa Ana and north, south, east, and west. All those streets and neighborhoods that looked exactly like each other, passing so many tract developments that weren't named Willows Village but could be. So many restaurants to stop at or drive through and eat so much food in, so many stores to shop in, so many gas stations to get gas. I wore the new shirt and a tie Aunt Maggy gave me, even a sports coat I told her I would only borrow, and I'd gone back twice to those dealers and one more that I thought maybe about, too, but nobody called back. My good mom sent me money by Western Union fast, no questions. I didn't need it that way but it was what she wanted. I felt bad about it. I didn't like it. She didn't want me to have to borrow or take anything from her sister. I think she felt jealous and she didn't want Aunt Maggy to think she didn't have plenty, too. I felt bad asking for help, but what could I do? I did really believe that, especially that one used car place, that guy wanted to hire me. It was about me speaking Spanish. He didn't, none of his salesmen did. He said they really needed that because they got so many Spanish Mexican people. That's how he said it. He called me Guillermo and I thought that was fine if I got the job. Then again I wasn't sure of anything, since he hadn't called or the other place, either, when I felt like it was such a sure thing.

Yeah, it was strange to be in the pink girl's room. At first, to be polite, I didn't want to make any moves, any changes in it. The cute little pink and red and white pillows stayed in the bed with me when I slept. Then I stacked them in a corner of the bed, and then I left them in a pile off the bed, though I kept a couple, sort of extra cushions, for my feet, my head. I finally picked the TV up off the floor and put it on the sewing machine cabinet. Once, I started opening makeup compacts—she had so many in this one box. I was looking in the little mirrors when I started laughing at myself. What if someone saw me? Very very funny! I wondered what it'd be like to have to stare at my lips putting on gloss. I looked at the lines in my own lips. Funny! I pushed boxes around and made room for my suitcase, but I was neat, tried to be. My own clothes looked heavy and dark in the room on the floor. Even my socks. I'd spilled a perfume, or something like it, and the room really stank of it. At first I was embarrassed that I'd gotten it on the rug. But it didn't stain. Aunt Maggy didn't say anything about it. At first I kind of didn't like the smell, but then I did. By now I was sick of it, tired of it being in my nose when I slept. I thought it would go away fast, but it never seemed to. I even worried that I might have the smell on me or in my clothes, so one day, before I took off, I went into Aunt Maggy's bedroom when she wasn't there and I borrowed some of Jim's men's spray. I saw a couple of bottles on his dresser there when she took me up for ties and shirts. I was sick of that perfume smell in my room but what could I do?

I woke up and I didn't feel like going out there, so I fell back asleep and it was later in the morning. It was the first time this late in the morning that I was still here. When

I woke up this second time, a couple hours later, I needed to pee. I opened my door and, across, Aunt Maggy's doors were both open and she was standing near the king-size bed completely naked, drying her hair, looking toward the long mirror I couldn't see across the set of sinks on the wall over there. She didn't hear me open the door—she had a radio on—and so I closed it. Not all the way. I left it open enough to see. Oh my God my aunt was a Playmate of the Year! It was shocking to me, and I couldn't believe it. She was too much. I couldn't stop myself from looking, even though I knew it was sick, or something kind of bad, but I didn't want to not watch. She finally rolled her hair into the towel and then she sat to put panties on. Then she stood and put on a bra, kept playing with this or that around her breasts, but she didn't like it, so she took it off and dug in a drawer and then she found another. She kept this bra on, and when she went toward the sinks and mirrors, I closed the door and breathed and shook my head quietly for at least a minute. I didn't know what it would mean that I just watched my own aunt so much and so naked. No way she was an older woman! Though I felt like I'd done something wrong and gotten away with it, or maybe because I'd gotten away with it, I felt kind of good. Better than I did before, a lot. I made noise this time when I opened the door. The cabinet near the bathroom, where there were bath towels and linens, was open, so I took one out and closed the door hard and then I closed the bathroom door and I even took a shower. When I was out, she had closed one of the two doors, though the other was open like normal. I heard her downstairs, a TV set on, talking to Lorena.

★   ★   ★

I saw this guy painting a house a few houses from the Willows Village entrance and he said yeah, it would be great if I worked with him, so it was me and this Gabe. It was his mom's house and it was for sale and he wasn't really a house painter, either, but while we were working, first one, then another woman, in this village stopped and asked if we wanted more work. We both looked at each other and said sure. He bid what seemed to be a ton and we agreed to split it. We were knocking out his mom's so fast it was amazing. It's because the house was a single story and there wasn't that much brush or roller work. It was 95 percent compressor. Three days is all it took and when we did the next one we both knew it would only take two, because now we knew how to do it and we had the drop cloths and all of it. The two-story we said yes to, also—but even that, well, we'd have to rent an extension ladder or maybe a scaffold, but after that, nothing to it, either. It wasn't like I was going to be rich, but it felt good to have some money and more coming. I even told Suzie and she felt better about me being out here, too. I didn't usually tell her anything that wasn't good, because I didn't want her to worry or to worry her parents, either—they didn't want her and their grandchildren to leave El Paso. I told her I was sure we'd get another couple before we finished and that soon I'd get a real job. I wasn't ready to give up. I just wanted the opportunity to make more money than I knew I ever could there.

On Saturday, Gabe and I drank a few beers, and I got back to Maggy's tired and I fell right asleep. I woke up at around three in the morning and I was hungry. I didn't want to treat her house like it was mine, so I never went into the refrigerator unless she said to. But I was hungry. I went downstairs and turned on those bright lights until I opened the refrigerator. There was light in it, so I could turn off the big ones. Then I looked inside. Impossible to know what was there because there was so much. Who ate so many pickles? I had never seen my aunt or Lorena eat one. And mustard jars. Who knew there were so many brands of mustard? Salsas in jars, so many, and I knew they would all be bad and I wondered if my aunt could eat them, too. I had to put things on the floor. I tried to be organized and quiet. So many things in foil that didn't look like food. One thing could have been beef once upon a time, and there was maybe a chicken, though it was too small and it smelled wrong. There was some ham and I thought that would be it. I started looking inside plastic cartons and I found some *chile* that tasted real next to some tamales that were rock hard. And then I found a plastic container with wide noodles. They had a white sauce on them and they were really good, too, and so then I was putting things away when Lorena, in a huge T-shirt, scared me.

"I wondered what that light was, so I had to wake up," she said.

"I was trying to be real quiet."

"You were, you were," she said. "It was one of the reasons I decided to get up and look, because it was just a light."

"Sorry."

"Don't say that. Did you find anything in there? She has so much."

"Really, huh?"

"It's that she never eats. She takes a bite, and that's it, in the fridge. But she wants everything anyway. What'd you find?"

"Noodles."

"Oh, those are the ones she made. She bought that pasta machine. She said Jim likes pasta." She shook her head and made a face. "And so she bought it and we made pasta one day. Like she'll ever do it again. It is really good. We ate some right after she made it, or I did. I forgot it was there. I'm the one who saved it. I'm also the one she told to."

I was standing, not sure how to eat it, since now eating seemed to involve Lorena, but she read my mind.

"With a fork, eat, stop thinking. She doesn't remember it's there, and she wouldn't care if she did."

"It is good," I said.

"Fresh. Fresh cheeses too. Always the best at Maggy's."

I poured a little *chile* on it.

"That's right, make it Mexican." She leaned against me as though she always did.

"What're you, anyway?"

"My dad's Greek. He barely speaks English. My mom's from Mexico, but she's half Greek, too. She grew up in a restaurant in Mexico City, but came here for college and never left."

"Greek. I would've never thought of it."

"Let's go sit. Bring your food."

She didn't mean the table, she meant the den where there was a couch. I sat. She lit a candle and then sat more close to me than I would've expected. I really loved the *chile*, as much as the noodles, and I decided I'd eat all these noodles, so I poured it all over them. Lorena laughed at that.

"How come you never come down and talk to me or watch television with me?"

"I don't know. It's my aunt's house." She'd scooted closer, and it was impossible not to like it. "I'm married. My wife's pregnant and we already have a daughter."

"I'm married, too," she said. "I still love my asshole husband."

I ate. She got closer to me and then she was leaning against me. The candlelight jumped from wall to wall. I finished and put the container on the table in front of me. Lorena cuddled against me after that. I could feel her so warm and then I put my arm around her on her shoulder and she kissed my neck. It made me have goose bumps. Then she started kissing me more and moving into me and we were kissing and her T-shirt was so warm and I started feeling her under it, too, and it didn't stop.

Gabe started getting moody with me. He wanted to get to this other job the next weekend. I'd proudly sent money to both my mom and Suzie from the one we just finished because I was expecting more. We had another house come up, too, and a few more people had asked about our prices and availability. He was being something and he wouldn't say why. I was starting to think. I didn't even know where he lived, and he never once asked me about where I lived, where my aunt was, on which street. I only knew where his mom used to live. I told him more than he told me. I was a little worried, too, because I told him about Lorena right after that night and I wished I hadn't. I don't think he was shocked or disapproving or anything. But he had that on me. It was then that I noticed it was more than a bad day. Not me, but him being selfish, and I didn't matter enough to get an explanation. He even left me alone for a long time and came back and no explanation for that, either. I was having to think what I would do if I didn't have this work. He had the phone numbers. He had a truck. I was hoping that the man who wanted the next house would drop by and I could get the job on my own.

"We've been kind of fighting, too," Lorena said when I got back. Aunt Maggy wasn't even there. "She drinks too much and she gets all bitchy."

"You drink a lot, too."

"Probably. But I don't get all bossy at her like she does me. It's not like her to go out alone. Usually she sends me on errands she doesn't want to do. When she takes me with her shopping, she always buys me something pretty. Lately she acts like that makes her mad, like I'm asking her to. I'm not. I don't care."

I was upset when I came in but Aunt Maggy was worse, like she was drinking the wine straight out of the bottle. It was like she was waiting for me to get here, even though I was so early.

"I had to ask Lorena to leave," she told me. "It is so disturbing."

"What happened?"

"She said horrible and mean things to me. I am still so upset." She drank from her wineglass.

"Were you guys drinking when this happened?"

"What do you mean by that?" She stood up. "I am not going to be criticized by you, too." She had her wineglass in her hand, but she put it down in the kitchen and paced around.

"I'm sorry," I said. "That's not what I meant."

She didn't want to listen. I went up the stairs, into the pink bedroom. I sure didn't want this. I didn't even ask about dinner, even though I was starving. It was the first time she didn't bring it up. I guess I was being punished. I would just go get something. I wanted to apologize, but I heard her go into her bedroom. She got on the phone, too. I was getting mad. Everything was making me mad. All these people had things, good jobs, everything. I was in the pink bedroom. I was thinking I should just go out. I was glad that Lorena was gone. That was a relief. I wanted to call Suzie. I wanted her to tell me she missed me and our baby was good. I wanted to talk to her about this work, about Gabe burning me. I couldn't tell her though. I didn't want to tell anybody, really, because I was embarrassed by how much trouble I was having. I didn't imagine this. I could go back to El Paso. I could say I didn't like it here. I didn't really. All of it made me mad and I was tired of the driving and the gas money. I was going to tell Maggy what happened and would have.

I went to a chain fast food place and I ate a chicken burger with jalapeños and fries and some bad iced tea. I called and I called that Gabe, but he didn't pick up and he was not going to pick up. I couldn't do anything, not one thing I could think of. I was thinking I would just go back to El Paso. I went back to the Willows Village. Aunt Maggy was around the corner from the kitchen and watching TV—I peeked around the corner and she never looked up, like she didn't even hear me come back in, though I knew she did. I went up to the pink room and thought of watching TV too, and packing up my clothes, but instead I started looking at those

photos she had everywhere, that I'd shoved under the bed
and put in an empty doll box. Pictures of so many people I
had never seen and not one of my family, of my mom or dad
but especially my mom. My mom, who talked about Maggy
all the time. Even if she was jealous of her, she admired her
like a hero and envied her life. I wondered if I should tell my
mom when I got back. So many photos of so many people
and so many families and not one of our own family. Where
did she get them all?

Then I heard Maggy's car go out of the garage, the
automatic garage door opening and closing. Since her room
looked over that driveway, I hurried to look out the window
to make sure it was her. It was nighttime, it was dark, but
she left a light on by the bed and that's where I saw what I
am sure nobody would ever see ever. It was a pile of bills, of
money. Not one that was stacked, in anyway organized, but
a crumpled pile. Each one crumpled in its own way, even,
individually. And it was a big pile, big as a birthday cake—no,
for a wedding. It was tall and it was wide. At first I just stared,
even as I got closer to it. I didn't want to disturb anything.
Since it was close to the edge of the bed, I went to my knees
like I was going to pray but only to get my eyes closer. It
was dark. I wasn't believing my eyes. They were hundred-
dollar bills. I couldn't imagine how many hundred-dollar bills
there were. It was uncountable to me maybe because I was
so nervous about being there and awed, both. I kept looking
to see if there were other bills besides hundreds, and it did
not seem like it, not one wasn't. She could not know how
many there were, it couldn't be possible. Hundreds of hundreds. It was more like she'd had these in a grocery bag and

dumped them all out onto the bed. I went ahead and picked one off, carefully, from the top. I couldn't believe it was real, that anyone would have so many, and then like this. Then I was thinking. And I did it. I took five of them. Because she wouldn't even know! And it didn't look even a little different after I did. It would be like taking five pennies from a jar of them. Then I went to the pink room. At first I was throwing my stuff around and bumping things. I wanted to pack my suitcase. I already wanted to leave before, but I needed the money and if she had so much, well, come on! I don't know how long I was more confused. I thought I shouldn't run out, like I did this. That I should wait a day or two but tell her as soon as I could that I decided I had to go back home, it just wasn't working out. Maybe the day after tomorrow. I don't know how much time passed but I was afraid she would be back any minute. I couldn't do it. I had uncrumpled them, but I crumpled three of them and rushed back in and ... it looked no different with or without those. I hoped it would make me feel better and it did, a little. Now I had gas money, I told myself. Enough to drive back and so I wouldn't have to borrow. The better feeling was for a few minutes, is all. So much I never did before Willows Village. I was trying to think smart. Because she wouldn't know. She would never know.

Then the automatic garage door was opening. It was done, there was no turning back. I closed the pink bedroom's door and I turned on the TV and I sat on the bed like it was a couch. I wasn't watching or listening to it, only for her, to hear her. I think I heard her in the kitchen. I think I heard her coming up the stairs. And then she knocked on the door. I got up and said come in at the same time.

She didn't say anything at first. "I know I have so many of those. Probably drives you crazy, doesn't it?"

I was holding one of her dolls. I didn't even realize. "It accidentally fell onto the bed from above and I guess I didn't put it right back." I tossed it back on the bed.

"Well, it seems like you," she joked.

I nodded, more ashamed than embarrassed. I looked over at the doll like I shouldn't have tossed it like I did.

"I want to apologize to you," Aunt Maggy said.

"For what?"

"Today. I was upset about Lorena."

"I understand. It makes sense. I'm sorry, too."

"Should I close this?" She was talking about the bedroom door.

"I guess, yeah."

It was just about closed. "Oh," she said, reopening it. "I think you have good news. A phone message. It was a man asking for Guillermo."

"That car dealer," I said. "One of them."

"I think so. Do you know how to listen to the messages on the machine?"

"I can figure it out."

"Goodnight then," she said, and she closed the door.

His Birthday

There was traffic on his birthday. The Hollywood Freeway to downtown. His father got off and got back on going in the opposite direction and then on again saying he'd catch the 5 Freeway and then, when they got there, the ramp was closed for repair. His father wasn't as loud as it was outside the open windows—cars and trucks and motorcycles, engines and tires, the gray city roar—but anyone could hear him say how he should have thought of this traffic before and that he shouldn't have promised to go to the store so far away and that he couldn't understand how people could live like this all the time. At home nothing was like here, he said. When he was small, he didn't have toys like they have now, and he didn't expect them. Maybe they should go somewhere else, his mother said, to any shopping center where a toy store was open. His father said she should have called around like people who used phones. She glared back at him, mad. The boy was six today. As they drove home his body slumped into the backseat.

Then his father accelerated, said they were going, he said they'd go. It seemed his father drove faster. He made one turn, then another turn, and then the Glendale Freeway and the 5 Freeway. His father said today was his son's birthday. Here, they were here. Now the boy was on his feet, hanging over the front seat between his parents. His mother was worried if something wasn't right still. Was this right? Was he sure they shouldn't turn back, or maybe they wouldn't recognize it, or maybe they'd gone too far? Then his mother said wait, over there. There was a drawing of a giraffe on the building. Unless it was the zoo, she said. His father laughed at his mother. You're the zoo, he said. No, you are, she said. His baby brother was excited and pointed, and his baby sister still slept. The boy controlled his body but not his smile. They were there! They parked in the oil-puddled lot and set up a collapsible stroller, the freeway howling beside them, and, pushing the thick glass doors, they went inside the store.

It was at least twelve feet high with toys, a warehouse, more toys than all the days of childhood, all squeals and squeaks and putts, boys and girls running and whining, bouncing and rolling things. His father and his mother and the two boys and the baby sister were each twisting their necks and stopping, look at this, look at this. Get anything you want, his father told him, but he didn't say but not for too much. He couldn't talk about money on his son's birthday, didn't want to explain about paying bills, the other expenses, worries, how it was away from home. There's so many things, the boy said, it's so hard. Well, get what you want, that one you wanted. I just don't know if it's the best one, the boy said, and his father said oh yes it is, it's the best one, and his father thought that the price was right, too, and he said it's got 145 pieces and a big mountain, and tanks, and a landing craft to cross the river, and fighter planes. The boy wanted to know who the good guys were and who were the bad guys and how could you tell? His father shook his head, you just know. And the boy smiled and his father found a new unopened box almost as tall as the boy who glowed. They were all ready to go home but his mother wanted to buy some party plates and his brother had to get something so he didn't cry, so they chose an $.87 package of horses and for his baby sister a soft, pink braceletlike teething ring for $1.19. They stood in line to pay. There were long lines. The boy waited contentedly, but the other two could not and his mother took them away. The boy stared at his box, at the pictures, and his father stood there and waited with all the other waiting people. When they got near the register, someone asked if it was always crowded like this, and a woman nodded, saying life in the big city. His father paid next, and the boy pulled the box off the counter, I want to carry it myself, and everyone in the family seemed as happy as him.

At home, his mother stabbed six candles into the brown frosting. It was chocolate devil's food with three white flowers and green leaves and white spiraled frosting, in longhand, Happy Birthday! She arranged the candles so there were five blue ones at each corner of an imaginary star and one yellow one in the middle. His father posed the boy next to the cake and took a picture, then she found some matches and lit the candles, and then his mother and father sang, only their voices, his father's gruff, his mother's soft, the baby girl in her arms, the younger boy, eyes wide open. It was overcast outside the window near this. The man next door who nagged and screamed at his wife was sweet-talking his dog, and there was a police helicopter swirling around and black-and-whites filling up the street behind them. A radio not so far away screamed a love song by Yolanda del Río. The father snapped a picture with a flash of the boy blowing out the candles. His mother brought out two more presents, each wrapped in paper that had been around the house, without ribbon or bows. She said, the little one's from your brother and sister, the big one's from your mami and papi. The little one was comics and the boy smiled, so happy, and he grabbed the other and ripped it open. It was a plastic sword, and now he was happy beyond words. His mother cut up the cake and his father scooped out ice cream and they all sat around quietly eating off the party plates. The radio outside wasn't on. Instead they heard a police bullhorn mumbling on the street behind them. His father told the boy to wait a minute, he thought he had a couple of batteries. He loaded them in the black plastic handle of the sword, and then handed it to the boy. The six-year-old held it above his head with both hands and lit up the yellow plastic blade. Slicing the darkening air, his whole family admired him as he swirled in the center of the room, brave and fearless.

UNCLE ROCK

In the morning, at his favorite restaurant, Erick got to order his favorite American food, sausage and eggs and hash-brown *papitas* fried crunchy on top. He'd be sitting there, eating with his mother, not bothering anybody, and life was good, when a man started changing it all. Lots of times it was just a man staring too much—but then one would come over. Friendly, he'd put his thick hands on the table as if he were touching water, and squat low, so that he was at sitting level, as though he were so polite, and he'd smile, with coffee-and-tobacco-stained teeth. He might wear a bola tie and speak in a drawl. Or he might have on a tan uniform, a company logo on the back, an oval name patch on the front. Or he'd be in a nothing-special work shirt, white or striped, with a couple of pens clipped onto the left side pocket, tucked into a pair of jeans or chinos that were morning-clean still, with a pair of scuffed work boots that laced up higher than regular shoes. He'd say something about her earrings, or her bracelet, or her hair, or her eyes, and if she had on her white uniform, how nice it looked on her. Or he'd come right out with it and tell her how pretty she was, how he couldn't keep himself from walking up, speaking to her directly, and could they talk again? Then he'd wink at Erick. Such a fine-looking boy! How old is he, eight or nine? Erick wasn't even small for an eleven-year-old. He tightened his jaw then, slanted his eyes up from his plate at his mom and not at the man, definitely

not at this man he did not care for. Erick drove a fork into
a goopy American egg yolk and bled it into his American
potatoes. She wouldn't offer the man Erick's correct age,
either, saying only that he was growing too fast.

She almost always gave the man her number if he was
wearing a suit. Not a sports coat but a buttoned suit with a
starched white shirt and a pinned tie meant something to her.
Once in a while, Erick saw one of these men again at the
front door of the apartment in Silverlake. The man winked at
Erick as if they were buddies. Grabbed his shoulder or arm,
squeezed the muscle against the bone. What did Erick want
to be when he grew up? A cop, a jet-airplane mechanic, a
travel agent, a court reporter? A dog groomer? Erick stood
there, because his mom said that he shouldn't be impolite. His
mom's date said he wanted to take Erick along with them
sometime. The three of them. What kind of places did Erick
think were fun? Erick said nothing. He never said anything
when the men were around, and not because of his English,
even if that was what his mother implied to explain his silence. He didn't talk to any of the men and he didn't talk
much to his mom, either. Finally they took off, and Erick's
night was his alone. He raced to the grocery store and bought
half a gallon of chocolate ice cream. When he got back, he
turned on the TV, scooted up real close, as close as he could,
and ate his dinner with a soup spoon. He was away from all
the men. Even though a man had given the TV to them. He
was a salesman in an appliance store who'd bragged that a
rich customer had given it to him and so why shouldn't he
give it to Erick's mom, who couldn't afford such a good TV
otherwise?

When his mom was working as a restaurant hostess and was going to marry the owner, Erick ate hot fudge sundaes and drank chocolate shakes. When she worked at a trucking company, the owner of all the trucks told her he was getting a divorce. Erick climbed into the rigs, with their rooms full of dials and levers in the sky. Then she started working in an engineer's office. There was no food or fun there, but even he could see the money. He was not supposed to touch anything, but what was there to touch—the tubes full of paper? He and his mom were invited to the engineer's house, where he had two horses and a stable, a swimming pool, and two convertible sports cars. The engineer's family was there: his grown children, his gray-haired parents. They all sat down for dinner in a dining room that seemed bigger than Erick's apartment, with three candelabras on the table, and a table-cloth and cloth napkins. Erick's mom took him aside to tell him to be well-mannered at the table and polite to everyone. Erick hadn't said anything. He never spoke anyway, so how could he have said anything wrong? She leaned into his ear and said that she wanted them to know that he spoke English. That whole dinner he was silent, chewing quietly, taking the smallest bites, because he didn't want them to think he liked their food.

When she got upset about days like that, she told Erick that she wished they could just go back home. She was tired of worrying. "Back," for Erick, meant mostly the stories he'd heard from her, which never sounded so good to him: She'd had to share a room with her brothers and sisters. They didn't have toilets. They didn't have electricity. Sometimes they didn't have enough food. He saw this Mexico as if it were the backdrop of a movie on afternoon TV, where children walked around barefoot in the dirt or on broken sidewalks and small men wore wide-brimmed straw hats and baggy white shirts and pants. The women went to church all the time and prayed to alcoved saints and, heads down, fearful, counted rosary beads. There were rocks everywhere, and scorpions and tarantulas and rattlesnakes, and vultures and no trees and not much water, and skinny dogs and donkeys, and ugly bad guys with guns and bullet vests, who rode laughing into town to drink and shoot off their pistols and rifles, as if it were the Fourth of July, driving their horses all over town like dirt bikes on desert dunes. When they spoke English, they had stupid accents—his mom didn't have an accent like theirs. It didn't make sense to him that Mexico would only be like that, but what if it was close? He lived on paved, lighted city streets, and a bicycle ride away were the Asian drugstore and the Armenian grocery store and the corner where black Cubans drank coffee and talked Dodgers baseball.

When he was in bed, where he sometimes prayed, he thanked God for his mom, who he loved, and he apologized for not talking to her, or to anyone, really, except his friend Albert, and he apologized for her never going to church and for his never taking Holy Communion, as Albert did—though only to God would he admit that he wanted to because Albert did. He prayed for good to come, for his mom and for him, since God was like magic, and happiness might come the way of early morning, in the trees and bushes full of sparrows next to his open window, louder and louder when he listened hard, eyes closed.

★   ★   ★

The engineer wouldn't have mattered if Erick hadn't told Albert that he was his dad. Albert had just moved into the apartment next door and lived with both his mother and his father, and since Albert's mother already didn't like Erick's mom, Erick told him that his new dad was an engineer. Erick actually believed it, too, and thought that he might even get his own horse. When that didn't happen, and his mom was lying on her bed in the middle of the day, blowing her nose because she didn't have the job anymore, that was when Roque came around again. Roque was nobody—or he was anybody. He wasn't special, he wasn't not. He tried to speak English to Erick, thinking that was the reason Erick didn't say anything when he was there. And Erick had to tell Albert that Roque was his uncle, because the engineer was supposed to be his new dad any minute. Uncle Rock, Erick said. His mom's brother, he told Albert. Roque worked at night and was around during the day, and one day he offered Erick and Albert a ride. When his mom got in the car, she scooted all the way over to Roque, on the bench seat, who was supposed to be her brother, Erick's Uncle Rock. Albert didn't say anything, but he saw what had happened, and that was it for Erick. Albert had parents, grandparents, and a brother and a sister, and he'd hang out only when one of his cousins wasn't coming by. Erick didn't need a friend like him.

What if she married Roque? his mom asked him one day soon afterward. She told Erick that they would move away from the apartment in Silverlake to a better neighborhood. He did want to move, but he wished that it weren't because of Uncle Rock. It wasn't just because Roque didn't have a swimming pool or horses or a big ranch house. There wasn't much

to criticize except that he was always too willing and nice,
too considerate, too generous. He wore nothing flashy or expensive, just ordinary clothes that were clean and ironed, and
shoes he kept shined. He combed and parted his hair neatly.
He didn't have a buzz cut like the men who didn't like kids.
He moved slow, he talked slow, as quiet as night. He only ever
said yes to Erick's mom. How could she not like him for that?
He loved her so much—anybody could see his pride when he
was with her. He signed checks and gave her cash. He knocked
on their door carrying cans and fruit and meat. He was there
when she asked, gone when she asked, back whenever, grateful. He took her out to restaurants on Sunset, to the movies in
Hollywood, or on drives to the beach in rich Santa Monica.

Roque knew that Erick loved baseball. Did Roque like baseball? It was doubtful that he cared even a little bit—he didn't
listen to games on the radio or TV, and he never looked at a
newspaper. He loved boxing, though. He knew the names of
all the Mexican fighters as if they lived here, as if they were
Dodgers players, like Steve Yeager, Dusty Baker, Kenny Lan-
dreaux, Mike Marshall, or Pedro Guerrero. Roque did know
about Fernando Valenzuela. Everyone did, even his mom,
which is why she agreed to let Roque take them to a game.
What Mexican didn't love Fernando? Dodger Stadium was
close to their apartment. He'd been there once with Albert
and his family—well, outside it, on a nearby hill, to see the
fireworks for Fourth of July. His mom decided that all three
of them would go on a Saturday afternoon, since Saturday
night, Erick thought, she might want to go somewhere else,
even with somebody else.

Roque, of course, didn't know who the Phillies were. He knew nothing about the strikeouts by Steve Carlton or the home runs by Mike Schmidt. He'd never heard of Pete Rose. It wasn't that Erick knew very much, either, but there was nothing that Roque could talk to him about, if they were to talk.

If Erick showed his excitement when they drove up to Dodger Stadium and parked, his mom and Roque didn't really notice it. They sat in the bleachers, and for him the green of the field was a magic light; the stadium decks surrounding them seemed as far away as Rome. His body was somewhere it had never been before. The fifth inning? That's how late they were. Or were they right on time, because they weren't even sure they were sitting in the right seats yet when he heard the crack of the bat, saw the crowd around them rising as it came at them. Erick saw the ball. He had to stand and move and stretch his arms and want that ball until it hit his bare hands and stayed there. Everybody saw him catch it with no bobble. He felt all the eyes and voices around him as if they were every set of eyes and every voice in the stadium. His mom was saying something, and Roque, too, and then, finally, it was just him and that ball and his stinging hands. He wasn't even sure if it had been hit by Pete Guerrero. He thought for sure it had been, but he didn't ask. He didn't watch the game then—he couldn't. He didn't care who won. He stared at his official National League ball, reimagining what had happened. He ate a hot dog and drank a soda and he sucked the salted peanuts and the wooden spoon from his chocolate malt ice cream. He rubbed the bumpy seams of his home-run ball.

Game over, they were the last to leave. People were hanging around, not going straight to their cars. Roque didn't want to leave. He didn't want to end it so quickly, Erick thought, while he still had her with him. Then one of the Phillies came out of the stadium door and people swarmed—boys mostly, but also men and some women and girls—and they got autographs before the player climbed onto the team's bus. Joe Morgan, they said. Then Garry Maddox appeared. Erick clutched the ball but he didn't have a pen. He just watched, his back to the gray bus the Phillies were getting into.

Then a window slid open. *Hey, big man*, a voice said. Erick really wasn't sure. *Gimme the ball, la pelota*, the face in the bus said. *I'll have it signed, comprendes? Échalo, just toss it to me.* Erick obeyed. He tossed it up to the hand that was reaching out. The window closed. The ball was gone a while, so long that his mom came up to him, worried that he'd lost it. The window slid open again and the voice spoke to her. *We got the ball, Mom. It's not lost, just a few more.* When the window opened once more, this time the ball was there. *Catch.* There were all kinds of signatures on it, though none that he could really recognize except for Joe Morgan and Pete Rose.

Then the voice offered more, and the hand threw something at him. *For your mom, okay? Comprendes?* Erick stared at the asphalt lot where the object lay, as if he'd never seen a folded-up piece of paper before. *Para tu mamá, bueno?* He picked it up, and he started to walk over to his mom and Roque, who were so busy talking they hadn't noticed anything. Then he stopped. He opened the note himself. No one had said he couldn't read it. It said, *I'd like to get to know you. You are muy linda. Very beautiful and sexy. I don't speak Spanish very good, maybe you speak better English, pero No Importa. Would you come by tonite and let me buy you a drink?* There was a phone number and a hotel-room number. A name, too. A name that came at him the way that the home run had.

Erick couldn't hear. He could see only his mom ahead of him. She was talking to Roque, Roque was talking to her. Roque was the proudest man, full of joy because he was with her. It wasn't his fault he wasn't an engineer. Now Erick could hear again. Like sparrows hunting seed, boys gathered around the bus, calling out, while the voice in the bus was yelling at him, *Hey, big guy! Give it to her!* Erick had the ball in one hand and the note in the other. By the time he reached his mom and Roque, the note was already somewhere on the asphalt parking lot. *Look*, he said in a full voice. *They all signed the ball.*

CHEAP

I'd called Ben López about dumping my old water heater for a new one. Since he couldn't do it, and his uncle Manny Aceves didn't have time either, Ben gave me the number for Luke's Construction. I don't know why it was surprising to me that Ben was buddies with a big white guy like Luke, but that was based only on my dating Ben's sister, the activist Chicana, years earlier. Ben did air conditioning, sold weed, and did a little plumbing on the side. He was right about Luke—he offered to do the job for what could only be called better than fair. He had to resheet the rotted floor, replace old valves, some copper tubing and fittings, and make three back-and-forths to Home Depot. He cussed to himself a couple of times—I heard that—but not much else. He got that new tank in right, dragged away the old one, and left the water heater closet in better shape than it'd been in since long before I owned the house. And he didn't ask for a dime extra. I considered offering more or tipping him. I didn't. It helped that I led him to believe I might want him for more work. A few days later, he brought me formal, printed-out contract bids on a new deck, on painting the outside of my house, and on installing new toilets and sinks I was thinking about. Truth was I only wanted to know what he would charge so I could compare that to what some *mexicanos* would charge me.

Over a year later, I wanted more. I still taught guitar. My
students kept getting more talented, though, more mature,
as my musical career rose. I'd won an obscure award, I had
CDs that very few listened to, let alone bought. Good news
was I no longer supported a poet girlfriend who didn't have
a job, smoked dope and watched TV until 3 AM, and insisted
on every meal out because she didn't like my cooking. So I
had more money. The bad news was that I was starting to go
blind. I could drive, but I couldn't see up close. As in read.
I couldn't paint the interior walls of my house. It wouldn't
seem like that should have anything to do with sight.

I called two Mexicans, who left business cards at my
door (I could use a magnifying glass), but both numbers
were out of service. I called friends to see if anyone knew
anyone, and I searched the Internet. All I got were expensive
estimates. I decided to check with Luke's Construction and
didn't remember why not first.

"I saw you in the paper," Luke said, excited. "I didn't
even know you were a musician."

"You read that article."

"That's the one."

I was never good about talking celebrity with anyone,
even my far-from-it version. But Luke was nothing but
impressed.

"Most everybody here in Austin plays guitar. You play
a twelve-string, right?"

"No."

"But don't you play Spanish?"

"It's a common misunderstanding."

"I thought it said that you learned from a Spanish gentleman."

"Okay, yes, the newspaper said the music descended from Andrés Segovia."

"There!"

"He's just a famous name they pull out, everyone always says . . ."

". . . And that night you were playing some new Spanish music."

"Not exactly new. It's cool you read the article." The newspaper story wove in a couple of the usual clichés but wrote it better than he read it. "I did pieces by Isaac Albéniz and Heitor Villa-Lobos, who isn't . . ."

". . . Spanish guitar music!" he said, cutting me off fast like it was a game show.

I'd learned it was easier to surrender rather than explain even a little—say, by mentioning not just Bach but John Williams. Why, and why go on? "Anyway, not a twelve-string," I told him.

"I would've swore," he said. "I thought for sure it was special twelve-string music."

He wanted to go on. I didn't. "Let me show you the rooms," I said.

Not really old, maybe in his midforties at most, his legs moved stiffly, and the boots that propped them up clacked loud against the wood floor of the hallway. In my bedroom he measured the floors roughly, then he taped the hall and my office studio and the other bedroom as we talked about the colors and trim. He tossed out a number for the work that was very low. I grabbed it, and we set it for the next week.

"I got a couple men that can knock this out fast," he said. "They won't bother you none, either."

"So that's with the paint, too?" I asked, not believing this really low bid was possible.

"Yes, sir. Take 'em a day."

"That's fabulous."

"You won't mind they're Mexican?"

His idea of *Mexican* ran as deep as his about music. "You're asking a Mexican if he minds if you hire Mexicans?"

"Just making sure. There's members of my church who do. They think they're making things worse in this country."

I was born and raised in El Paso. My grandfather was from Juárez, my grandmother from Parral. My father was a pachuco back in the day, and my mother barely stopped using a tortilla as her only eating utensil. I was the only one in the family of two brothers and two sisters and ten thousand cousins who journeyed away. The rest were within a ten-mile radius. Worse, I never took strangers, conversationally or otherwise, back there for a visit. Not even myself, for that matter.

"Sounds like that church needs some church lessons," I said.

"It saved me," Luke said, not noticing any criticism. "Been hard days, especially this last year. It's when I started going again."

"Bad out there for working people."

"Least I'm feeling a little better now, and it's because of the church. My wife up and left me and my daughter." He spoke to me like we were good friends, like I already knew these details of his life, if vaguely. He was settling in. "I got lost there for years drinking and being irresponsible. Then I just started praying for goodness."

I didn't expect others to tell me about their lives, either. "So you found your religion." I was simply polite.

"Came home," he corrected me. He could have been choking up some, his voice cracking, but I realized that it was his teeth, some dental issue. "I was raised up so much in it I never paid no mind. Even my name's proof. Didn't have no fourth brother John because there was only Matthew, Mark, and me, Luke."

I never talked to the Bible people who came to my door, either.

He waited to see if I knew the answer. "That's the first books of the New Testament."

I knew, I told him I did, and he was encouraged.

"You ever want to come, you'd be welcome."

"I'll keep on as a lapsed Catholic."

Either he didn't know what that meant, or he really did just ignore it. "Church is good for healing. You'd see."

"Kind of you to suggest, thanks for the offer," I said, glad he was leaving.

A week later he was back at eight in the morning, bringing along tarps, rollers and pans, brushes, cans of paint, and the two men, a father and son, Carlos and Uriel. Carlos didn't speak any English, so all the instructions from Luke went to Uriel. They were told to start in my bedroom, told how to move and cover the furniture, how not to spill the paint, where to use rollers and where brushes. They were talked to

not only as though they might not know any of this, but as
though they'd better remember once their boss left. When
he finished his instructions, Luke met me by the front door.
I wanted to be sure everything would be all right.

"I've fired Uriel five times now," he said. It didn't even
occur to him to lower his voice any. "He's a good worker
when he listens and ain't being lazy. Since Carlos is here, too,
I'm sure it'll be fine."

"Sounds great," I said.

"I'll check in on them in a while," he told me, missing
any sarcasm from me and adding on to what I'd overheard.
"I can bring a contract then if you want."

"Not necessary. I'll do it cash. Better for you, right?
For taxes."

He smiled. His teeth looked worse than they sounded.
"Who wants to help this federal government, right?"

He used the words *federal government* with the same added
inflection he did when he said *Mexican* before. And there was
that familiarity with it he offered me, like I was a member of
his church. I did not care for it.

"I'm real glad Bush is gone, too," I said to mess with him.

He didn't blink. "We're working our asses off, and just
look at where they got us at now."

In lots of ways, Luke was what I liked about Austin when
I first came here. Texas as I knew it growing up was what we
just called Mexican, what the college-educated called Chicano. That was El Paso, where nobody had anything or learned
much because nobody knew beyond what was visible, within
an eye's reach, which I learned young wasn't enough. I didn't
know what happened to me or when it did or why, but I heard

music that couldn't be seen and wasn't heard anywhere near home. And so I went until I was in Texas again: Now I had this gig in Austin, where even people like Luke liked people like me. And therefore I liked them back, these bigger-than-me country white boys, who drank beer as they smoked *mota* in their trucks and listened to Willie Nelson and got out to hear Dale Watson. When people visited, I'd take them to dinner at Threadgill's and dancing at the Broken Spoke. A city where someone like me could come from El Paso and someone like Luke would nod his head wistfully and tell me, like no one from there ever did, how beautiful it was. That, at least, was Luke back when he didn't have a paunch and rotting teeth and bad knees and not enough work.

Here was my dilemma: I was very happy about how little this job was going to cost me. I wasn't rich, but I wanted to live like a classy musician. I wanted these walls in my house to get painted for the best price, inexpensive being my favorite. I didn't want the paid work to involve talk of current events.

Once Luke was out the door, I went to see the men in my bedroom.

"*¿Se fue?* He leff?" Uriel asked. His father was covering the dresser, bed, and end table that had been pushed to the center of the room.

"Yeah, he took off," I told him in Spanish.

"Good," he said in Spanish, too, looking over to Carlos, who also stopped to acknowledge the change. "It's much better when he's not around."

I really didn't want to get into it. Uriel, more relaxed, looked at me now. "It looks beautiful, your house."

"Thank you. I like it, too."

"We'll do it good," said Carlos. "You don't worry."

Uriel had been taking down the art and photos I had on my bedroom walls. Like I'd never seen it, he showed me the portrait of Benito Juárez I had up, as well-known in Mexico as the classic one of Abraham Lincoln is here. I bought it framed, rustic, completely coated by fiberglass. It seemed particularly strange held in the air by this young *mexicano* in his faded, torn Dallas Cowboys T-shirt.

"A souvenir," I explained. It was a knickknack, not more.

Both stared at me, wanting more. Uriel asked where I was born. I told him. "He said you were from Spain."

I probably rolled my eyes, maybe shook my head. "No. Hardly." I told them. "You?" I asked.

"Nuevo León," said Carlos.

"Tamaulipas," said Uriel.

"Reynosa," said Carlos. He shook his head at his son. "We didn't live there much."

"How long you been in the States?" I asked.

"In Austin?" said Uriel. "Three years."

"Me, almost one year," said Carlos.

"It's okay?"

"Not too good here, more worse there," said Carlos.

"Hard everywhere now," I said.

"I had a good job for a while," said Uriel. "Now I have to work for this idiot."

Carlos shook his head at his son again.

I didn't want to go there. "Well, you need something, let me know."

I went into my studio, which, before I'd lived there, was just a bedroom. I didn't want to stay in the house, but I didn't feel I should leave, either. They didn't have transportation—Luke had dropped them off—so it wasn't even possible for them to grab goodies and run. I shut the door to be more private. Besides being where I practiced my music, the studio also served as my office. I went to my computer first, tried to read e-mail as well as I could, paid a couple bills online, called about an appointment, then finally gave in to some practicing that they would hear. I was perfecting "Fandango" by Joaquín Rodrigo for a recital in Chicago. I played for about an hour before I came out for air.

They weren't finished, but I liked what I saw. Uriel was doing the rolling, and Carlos was way ahead with a brush, getting corners.

"Your playing was very cool," Uriel told me.

"I have to practice," I said. I buried my discomfort. It was the same response I had with my own family, probably because my job was so arty, so unlike ordinary life—their life. I was no different in front of overly dressed people at performances.

"You're good," Uriel said. "Is that what you do? For your living?"

Carlos stopped to hear this.

I said yes.

"Not at clubs," he guessed, not knowing what else.

They both stared at me. "Like concerts, but me alone. With the guitar."

"*Muy padre*," said Uriel. "Where can we see you here?"

"Not much here." They both had stopped and were listening intently. They wanted me to tell them. "Easier would be when I'm in Mexico. I've been to Xalapa, Monterrey, Guadalajara. Bellas Artes, the palace—you know that?" I waited. Neither said anything. "Mexico City. That was the best of all, you wouldn't believe it."

"*La capital*," said Carlos. "Imagine it."

"No words," I said.

"*Que padre*," said Uriel. "Wow."

I didn't want there to be too long a pause. "Is that other color all right, you think? For the finish?"

They agreed it would look good. I suggested water and brought them each a bottle, cold from the refrigerator. Both chugged. "I've got more," I told Carlos as he finished. He shook his head. I went for another anyway, and Uriel followed.

"I've been thirsty since we got here," he said.

"You should have said."

We were at the *refri's* door. "The boss doesn't want us to bother nobody. A law."

I gave him a new bottle and took another for Carlos.

"Lots of rules," he said.

I didn't respond. He'd stopped at the threshold of the living room. "Can I go in?"

How could I say no?

"I love your art," he said. "I wanted to be an artist when I young."

"Difficult life."

"You did it, no? A musician?"

"With luck." I wanted to say random luck—my being born on this side, not over there. I was as much aware of that fortune of nature as I was of my rarity in my own family.

"I don't believe it." He didn't either. You could tell.

I told him about a few of the pieces. He's from Los Angeles. He's from Mexico City. She's from L.A., too. She's from Chicago. He's from Oaxaca. I didn't tell him they were artists I now knew. I didn't think about it much, either, but around someone like Uriel, I even heard myself.

"Francisco Toledo, who lives in Oaxaca. You've heard of him?"

"One of the most famous in Mexico."

He was proud of his information as if he owned it. "One time I saw an exhibit of his art."

"Incredible, how cool."

Uriel browsed my living room, staring at and even touching my collection of trinkets, respectfully, like a first time in a museum. When he'd done a full circle, we walked back to where Carlos was still rolling away before I gave him a fresh bottle of cold water.

By about one in the afternoon, I was done practicing and hungry. I opened the door and Carlos was right in the hallway with a roller and Uriel was brushing the last, farthest corner. He didn't stop as I stood there.

"This room's next, right?" Carlos said of my studio office.

"Yes, yes. I'm done. I'll get out of your way."

He took the long view of it, and I saw what he did—a ton of work to prep alone.

"Lots," I said. "Sorry."

He nodded tiredly. "*Ni modo*. We got it." They both seemed in a stern work mood. I decided I would go pick up something for lunch and eat in the living room. I could make a couple of phone calls while they finished. I got my wallet and grabbed my keys. I went out the front door without explanation.

I drove to ¡Burrito Burrito!, not because it was so cheap but because of the food. It was as good as any restaurant charging at least twice as much for the same item. And I liked that it was a drive-through—a former burger joint misnamed Hotdog's (one of the signs was still there)—and that the owner was aware of healthier food options. At least he told me he didn't use lard anymore. I drove past the menu sign with the decade-ago-broken intercom mic and stopped next to the window.

The owner bent to show his face and greet me with the side of his hand. "*Hola*, boss. *¿Un* bean an' cheese *sin mucho queso como siempre?*"

It is what I almost always ordered. Never almost. "*Porfa, sí,*" I replied. It was the least expensive burrito they had, that was true, but it was what I liked. There was so much bean inside, it was like getting two anyway.

He told his cook the order a step away from the window, standing straight. On my side, I already had three dollars folded between my finger and thumb. I hadn't been there much for a few years because my girlfriend didn't do drive-up. Once on my own again, he became as regular at the drive-up as I was. An older man, gray, even distinguished if not for the apron, I'd say he looked Hungarian, but only because he was stocky and balding, seemed ethnic and European. Friendly always, we sometimes talked a little, sometimes not at all. At the beginning, a year ago or even two by now, we'd talked more. But about him, never me, which was another plus for the place. He was from Tampico, and as I drove up on stifling hot South Austin days, he cooled me with nostalgic stories of the ocean and beach and wind. He looked like a cook, but he told me he was a retired pilot for an Iranian airline. He only worked here for his son, he said, to fill in. Over time I found he was never not there, and I never saw a son, and I wondered what the story really was. I sensed too much pride, and disappointment, involved—he didn't dress for a fast food occupation. And the more I'd come, the quieter he'd gotten.

"Yes, leave a little bit for the poor," I said as he put the dollars into his register. He'd taken my ones, and the final bill left three pennies. I never took them, but he always politely offered. I put leftover pennies in that tray by any restaurant's cash register, not just here.

There was a car behind waiting, so when I got my burrito, I left quickly and was back at my house after a few turns. It was after one thirty and Carlos and Uriel were still working. Only then did it occur to me that they hadn't stopped for lunch. The hall was done. They were in my studio, getting it ready to paint. When I asked, Uriel shook his head in irritation and looked away.

Carlos shrugged. "Soon."

"But it's almost two." I still had the brown bag with a bean-and-cheese in my hand. "You're not hungry?"

"Of course we're hungry," snapped Uriel. He wasn't exactly answering me.

"You can't stop? Take a break?"

"The boss brings us lunch," Carlos said. "Then we eat lunch."

"We have to do what the man says," said Uriel.

Carlos turned his head away from that comment, as if grains of dirt would scratch his eyes.

I didn't feel I could eat if they didn't. I was sure they hadn't taken a break earlier either, that they'd been working straight since the morning. This wasn't the most exhausting work, no doubt, but still, at least lunch. I decided I had to drive back to ¡Burrito Burrito!

While I waited behind two cars ahead of me, I ate most of the bean burrito.

"*Buenas*, boss. You forget the pennies?"

That threw me off a second or two, as though something whizzed by the back of my head, just missing. "Well, you know, maybe give me two of carne asada."

Bent into the window, he stared at me curiously. "Tacos?"

I stared back at him, with curiosity. Of course he might have thought that I'd returned still hungry, but it didn't seem only that.

"Or burritos?" He waited. I was about to say, then he went on. "It's that the burritos are much bigger."

Like I wouldn't know the difference? I couldn't locate the tone yet, either.

"And," he finally said, attaching a smirk, "they cost much more than the tacos."

"Burritos," I said. I was about to explain, too, like I had to.

"Two? Really? You're throwing it around today, aren't you?"

He stood up and told his cook my order. Even that was with equal parts amusement and scorn that was too easy for me to hear.

"No drinks, right?" he asked.

"No . . ." I was about to tell him that I had bottled water.

". . . No, of course," he interrupted, sneering.

My body didn't seem willing to believe what it was hearing.

He came back with the price. It was about eleven dollars. Fact? It was the most I'd ever spent there in about two years. Still, that was no excuse, was it?

The change was a quarter. He handed me that, then the bag with the two burritos. "*Salsita roja* inside, napkins, all there." Then he offered me his *gracias muchas, aquí para servirle* with a bow, as always, gracefully, with a regal wave of the back of his hand.

I got back to my house with the burritos faster than I think I should have unless I speeded. I had processed what I actually did see and hear and moved over to what I should have said or done, other than sit there in my car, mute and limp.

"Here is food," I said to Carlos and Uriel. "You need to eat lunch." I was churning about myself. "I got carne asada for you," I mumbled, meaning not chicken or vegetarian—an Austin-only concern. I brought them both bottles of water, cold out of the *refri*. I still had some of my own burrito to eat, but I no longer wanted it. I wanted to go back there—to say and do what? I wanted to never go back there. I wanted, I didn't want.

They both sat, one against my studio door, the other
the jamb, peaceful, eating. They liked the food from there,
like I did. I was full of rage and hurried to my living room
couch to brood. I wanted to play guitar, but I couldn't with
them here. I couldn't listen to a book on tape. I dug around
for CDs and chose a Bach, the calming, faraway German. I
didn't want to get earphones from my studio. I tried not to
play it loud, definitely not as loud as I wanted.

Fifteen minutes later, Uriel was at the edge of my living room, as though it were darker there. He was keeping
a respectful distance, unsure when or if he should speak. I
told him to come and then I turned it down and said again
to come. *Pase, pase.* When it seemed he couldn't hear me, I
turned the music way down.

"Thank you," he said. "For the food."

Carlos shadowed him, saying thank you, too, but without the words. I'd probably made them uncomfortable. They
might have thought I was mad at them. I turned off the CD
with the remote.

"You had to eat. I can't believe you don't stop for lunch."

"He doesn't want us to until he comes here," said Uriel.

"You're supposed to take lunch."

Uriel looked over at his dad. "What I say."

"So it's going all right?"

"Good, very good," said Uriel.

"You'll be done? Today?"

Carlos nodded his head emphatically.

"We have the two rooms is all," said Uriel, "and the trim."

"That goes fast," Carlos told his son, "if we go." He
meant back to work instead of talking.

Which Uriel didn't want yet. "I love this room. Everything you have in it."

"I told Luke I wanted to paint it, too. This one, and that dining room, and that one little room over there."

Uriel stepped more into the living room and walked to the others. So did Carlos.

"We could do it," Uriel said. Carlos nodded.

"You mean," I said, "without Luke?"

"Yes, without the asshole," said Uriel. Carlos grimaced. The middle man cut out. He probably took as much as them combined.

"We could come Saturday, right?" said Uriel. Carlos nodded his head. "We need the work."

"He doesn't give you that much?" I asked.

"After this one, I have something else, but not my dad. He pays me weekly, but my dad is only by the day, for this job."

"I need to work," said Carlos.

"He doesn't pay you by the hour?"

Uriel squeezed his teeth and shook his head. "It's why I am always trying to get another." He turned bitter. "*Es muy pinche, el pendejo.*"

This time Carlos didn't disapprove of his son's disrespect calling Luke a *pinche*—"fucking cheap." "*Muy mezquino,*" he corrected. His a more refined version, more "tightwad" in meaning.

"*Un pinche mezquino,*" Uriel said. Carlos didn't smile, but he didn't frown, either.

"I can't believe he doesn't pay you by the hour," I repeated. "I sort of told him already I'd give him the job if this other came out well."

"We get here Saturday morning," said Uriel, "and paint it for you." Less forcefully, he suggested a figure to his dad. Carlos nodded. "We divide the money."

It was a lot less than what anyone else bid, including Luke.

"You have all the things you need? The drop cloths, brushes, rollers?"

"Of course."

He stared at me. I bet that meant he had Luke's things, but I decided not to ask. "So you don't say we talked."

He nodded his head, agreeing.

"What about the paint?" I asked.

That was a little problem since I wanted three different colors, but then Uriel dropped their price even more—my guess was by more than the cost of four gallons of paint—but now I would have to run to Home Depot and buy it.

"So, I'm going to tell him I want to wait on these rooms when he asks. That I have to do it later."

They both nodded, happy for the work and for the opportunity to screw Luke. I took Carlos's phone number, and they disappeared into my studio. I'd half forgotten about the incident at the burrito place. I turned on the stereo again, but listened to a radio station's music, and not very loud. The phone rang. I answered and talked.

Not an hour later, Luke rang the doorbell but walked right in. "Hey!" he yelled. "I made it." His boots seemed wet. Or maybe it was grease, smeared. They weren't work boots, they were cowboy boots he worked in. He had on a ragged Western shirt with snap buttons. Big, he seemed bigger than he even was right then. He was carrying a Whataburger bag. He didn't stop to say anything to me, clomping the hardwood floor, and turned and clomped and turned again into the studio.

"This is where you're at?" he said. He wasn't trying to be loud, his voice just was. Uriel said something. "Well, after you eat I need you to pick it up." Uriel said something. "I don't mean that, no! I mean go faster, *vámonos* faster, get the work done."

I was standing away from this, stopped where I did when I'd gotten up to answer the front door. First Luke reappeared, irritated. Behind him was Carlos, then Uriel, both of them eyeing me privately as they passed and went outside.

"They're gonna get done today, don't worry," Luke told me.

It hadn't occurred to me.

"I have to stay after them. Uriel, anyway. Fired him five times now." He shook his head.

Luke followed me into the kitchen. Through the window I could see them seated outside the front door eating the burgers and fries, a cold drink there, too.

"You've hired him back five or six times? He can't be all bad."

"If I watch him," he said. "Carlos being with him seems better at least."

"Maybe put Carlos on full-time, too. I'm sure he'd take it."

"Don't got that much work. I get it both ways. Either I don't got enough, or when I do, you got the federal government nosing in."

Irritated, I took the bait. "You mean the FBI or IRS investigates your violations?" Immigration was the word I was really saying. Called ICE now, before it was just *la migra*.

He wasn't sure what I meant, but, again, he assumed we thought alike. "You know, all this goddamn federal government intervention. . . ."

"And *Mexicans*, right?"

". . . and socialist takeover." He was so deep inside his own head, he didn't let any outside thoughts interfere. His mouth was even slurring worse than usual because the words were coming so fast. "He won't stay in office. Who's he think he is? Who's he think we are?"

"You mean that *nigger*?" I snapped.

There was no missing what I said this time. I was mad and I made him mad back, and he wanted to yell at me or lecture or preach, but he shut up. I hadn't paid him yet.

I sat down at my kitchen table, where I could see out the window Uriel and Carlos finishing their burgers. "Look," I said. "I want the work done in my house."

"It's what I do."

"I'm a musician, and it's all I ever do. I've been real lucky." I didn't do this, but I wanted to, I had to say more "You and me are lucky to be born on the rich side of a border."

Luke was standing high over me. What I'd said didn't throw him off a beat. "You're not so lucky," he told me.

"What's that supposed to mean?"

"What you're going through."

"What?" I stood up like we were about to throw blows —or I was. He seemed unaffected. "What're you talking about?"

"You know," he said. "I read about it." He used that familiar voice again, like he knew me, I knew him.

"Read about what?" I was certain he was about to bring up a couple of the stories about me and a crazy stalker who drove me out of L.A., a personal mess so many years ago. I still hated when anyone mentioned any of it still, anytime, but with the Internet, it was timeless public domain.

"The blindness," he said.

Stunned. My breath wasn't interacting with the room's air.

"It's what I read."

I sat down.

"It must be hard. Can you play your guitar without seeing?"

I didn't look up.

"I don't mean not seeing nothing. You must. You know what I mean. I don't really know how bad you got it. Seems like you're okay to me."

I mostly didn't think about any of this. I mostly went on not letting it matter so much to me or alter almost anything I did. Mostly I tried to ignore it. I dwelled on how far I'd made it, my good fortune.

"Right?" Luke asked. "That you do pretty okay with it? You see good enough, seems."

"You read about this?" I asked him.

"Yeah," he told me. "It's gotta be tough."

I wanted to ask him where he read it, but I didn't want to know. I stood up again. I didn't want any more conversation.

"Hey, listen," Luke said. "There's a woman at my church. She could help you out. She cleans houses, too. She could do lots of things for you, whatever you need. She's a very religious lady."

"Not necessary," I said.

"I don't mean you're a handicapped or nothing."

"So she's not Mexican, right?"

"No. Nothing but English." It was as though he hadn't heard me before, or what had happened was so far in the past that he'd already forgotten. "She gets going and she talks your ears off, I warn you. But she needs work."

"You worry about her."

"We try to take care of each other. Church has been good for me, like I told you."

The front door opened—Carlos and Uriel coming back to work—and Luke shifted his attention, clomping toward them. One of them flushed the toilet in the bathroom.

"Now listen, you both," he said, loud again. "You gotta get a move on." Uriel muttered something. "Well, you ate your *lonche* now, Uriel, so you can't bitch that that's holding you back." He went into the other bedroom and talked from there, raising his voice a little so Uriel could hear him. "You get done in there, this one should go fast." More boot steps down to my bedroom, then on to the studio, until finally where I was waiting, by the kitchen window.

"They're on schedule if they keep at it. I thought those trim colors you picked you'd be sorry about, but you saw good on 'em." He caught himself using the *see* verb.

I nodded.

"You got nothing to worry about. They'll have it done today."

"I appreciate it," I said.

"I'll be back in a bit. You think you might be interested in that housecleaning, let me know."

I didn't offer one more word.

I drove to the bank to get cash and to kill time out of the house. It did not cross my mind that Luz would be working the drive-up window. Luz was young, not as much in years, and I was old, not only in years. I'd gone out with her because she was really cute and sexy and she flirted with me—and I was a guy. But then it seemed she liked me too much. Not in that stalker way, but a lot more than a dinner out and fooling around in. She called a lot, was always wanting to come by or for us to go out or stay in but at least talk on the phone (where am I, what am I doing, don't I want her, don't I miss her?), and I just had to stop it. It'd become too much for me. I didn't like that she could see my bank accounts. That seemed wrong. I considered changing banks, but time passed, and it didn't matter. I thought the inside tellers were never near this car lot full of tubes.

Miss Garza had to say good afternoon twice to me, the second time with some exaggeration, so I'd catch on. "Oh, it's the lucky window," I said to the intercom when I figured it out. Truth was, I was too far away from their glass booth and I couldn't see her face. I didn't know if she could see mine.

"Yes it is."

"How are you, Lucita?"

"Okay."

"Just okay?"

"Still working here," she kind of whispered. She always wanted a much better job.

"I thought they kept all the hot women inside."

"At least you still think I'm hot."

"Like I or anybody could stop."

"Would you like hundreds, sir?" she said more loudly.

"Yes, ma'am."

Back to more a whisper. "So you *do* still remember me, then."

"Let me think."

"I'm never like what I was with you," she said quietly. "I don't know if I should be embarrassed or pissed at you."

"Is it all right to be talking like this here?"

"Only one of the girls next to me listens, and she's inside checking on something."

I heard the cylinder shooting down the vacuum tube. I opened the bank container. My check card was there, my license, a pen. "Uhh, I think you forgot my money, Miss Garza."

"Oh shit!" she said. Then she was laughing and trying to make herself stop. "I said *oh shit!*" she finally got out. Funny, more fun was to hear her laugh breaking up through the intercom. "You're gonna get me fired!"

"You should've gotten more hundreds out of me first."

"I'm still your cheap date," she said. "I am sure you remember *that*, mister!"

That got me laughing.

The cylinder shot back again, this time with the cash. "All here this time. I'm painting the house . . . paying somebody else to."

Louder. "Will that be all I can help you with today?" Meaning the other teller next to her was back.

"Thank you very much, Miss Garza," I said.

I expected her to say more, and I waited for it. I pushed the TALK button. "Hello?"

"Very nice to see you again, sir. I hope you have a good afternoon."

"Oh," I said. "It was . . ."

"I can't talk," she said fast, close to her mike.

So I took it out of park, and drove toward a different day. The laughing? Missing her naked? Her? I grinned, I breathed in, I turned up the car radio. Though no doubt she had a boyfriend, I wanted to take Luz to this Ozomatli concert being promoted. I turned left instead of right. I wasn't going fast or slow, it wasn't busy or not, and then a postcard invite: Surrounded by blue, the sun was centered above a thick mist of white cloud.

I pulled over and I got out and started on a caliche horse trail to the creek. At its edges, river-smoothed rocks were beside limestone boulders, their rusty geologic holes making them seem decorative. Next to them were nopal, barrel, yucca, and agave cactus, thorny weeds and cedar shrub, mesquite and oak tree, bushes that I knew bloomed pollen-heavy flowers that were yellow and red and cream. Ants were swarming the carcass of an armadillo—and near that I found a fossil, curled into itself, as big as my hand! My broken eyes wouldn't stop panning for more when I reached the creek, green as moss. I took off my shoes and rolled up my jeans, made a seat a few feet in on a boulder the river gave room. So many wild birds singing patterns, the wind and water currents humming backup. I tapped small rocks together to imitate the frogs, and I swore they replied. Hawks coasted above. Not far, over there, turkey vultures circled tighter. The whole cycle.

★   ★   ★

They still had half of the last bedroom to do. They both looked tired, but Carlos seemed especially squeezed dry, his chest hair poking through his thin undershirt. He was in the bathroom, at the tub, washing out the rollers, pans, brushes. The radio that was in the bedroom was on loud. A ranchera station.

"We'll get this tomorrow," Uriel said. "And Saturday? Did he say anything?'

"I didn't tell him anything yet, and he didn't ask."

"That's good. We can use the money."

I wished they'd finished and weren't coming back to-morrow. I was having second thoughts about Saturday now, not because I didn't want the rooms painted, but because I was confused.

"Listen, what if it wasn't this Saturday? Maybe a week or two."

He looked at me with such disappointment. "Better right now," he said.

"What the fuck?" It was Luke turning the corner of the hall. None of us heard him come in the front door. "Uriel, turn off that fuckin' music, you hear me?" Hard to imagine that we didn't hear him because his boots now seemed the only sound other than his voice. Noticing Carlos in the bathroom without missing a step, he went by me like I wasn't there at all. "You're not done in here? How is it you're not done in here, Uriel?" Uriel might have answered, but Luke wasn't interested in an explanation. "Goddamn if you won't finish this right now! What the hell you doing? You think you should leave when you only got another half hour of shit to do? Not if you wanna work for me!"

Carlos had come out of the bathroom. Uriel was moving his head, stepping sideways and back, his hands at each side, not making fists, not not making them, either. He told Carlos and Carlos didn't hesitate to want to jump back in. He got a roller and a paintbrush from the bathroom.

"Not that, goddamn it," Luke said, taking the pan but not roller. "Open that new one right there! Can't use one that's wet." He bent, opening paint cans like he was stabbing one of them. "Amount of time you two wasted cleaning up you'd been finished." Then he stood up, staring at Carlos, who was frozen. "What the fuck you waitin' for? Get a move on it!"

Uriel took the brush from his father and explained in Spanish. Luke stood over them, silent, like he was watching from a high mountain, as the two grown men scurried.

Front row to the drama, I thought one of them would attack Luke any minute, or should, though it was also true I was relieved that they were going to finish. Then my phone rang. I ran into my office, hoping it was Luz. Of course it wasn't. It was business, which I didn't want to talk, but no stopping it once I answered. When I finally got off, I started to dig around for Luz's phone number, the one not on my new cell phone. Should I give her the fossil I found? Tell her how I was, what was happening? Tell her: Such beauty in the world, and I miss it until the ants catch my attention. I laughed at myself. She would have no idea what I was talking about if it made sense! But she would love the fossil —who wouldn't?—and, really, that was the gift.

Right then I noticed what a good job Uriel and Carlos had done in the studio, not just painting, but putting everything back where it was. It was like they'd copied a photograph—didn't misplace a book, a sheet of music, or an envelope that I'd aimed at the trash can and missed. It was the same in my bedroom, which I hadn't looked at since the morning. I'd almost believe they changed the sheets before they made the bed.

"I want to apologize," Luke told me in the kitchen.

"Hey," I said, drinking some water, "it's one of those days." It was close to six in the evening.

"I feel bad for using the Lord's name in vain. Trying to stop that."

"And I thought you were apologizing about how you were around those men."

"I do. But they should be finished in a minute, I can promise you that. I was plenty mad. I am about to be making this the last time with Uriel. No more."

He misunderstood, like someone who was still learning a new language. "They've done a great job," I told him.

"I don't know what we gonna do, I don't."

It was his big *we* again. I wanted him to go.

"What I gotta live in, what's breathing down my neck, is where there's nothing for people like me, that's what I'm telling you."

"You need some water?" I said.

"Don't mind if I do," he said.

I got a glass out of a cabinet and filled it from the tap, and he drank it steadily. I completely forgot about the cold water I had in the refrigerator.

"We finish, Luke." Uriel was at the kitchen's threshold.

Luke shook his head. He put down the glass, shook his head.

Uriel angled to let Luke pass by. When he had, Uriel looked at me, made eyes, shook his head. Then he turned and followed, as brave as he was humiliated. I could hear Luke in there, and he was not yelling. The boots clomped back toward me.

"It's all I got now," he said, coming back into the kitchen, leaning onto the counter, tired. Uriel and Carlos were already behind him, moving tarps and things out.

I'd gotten my wallet out.

"Did you want a receipt?"

"Won't be necessary, no."

"Way I like it, too. Keep them monkeys in suits out of it."

I forgot my count. He saw, held my gaze for a few seconds, then his eyes aimed down. I had to count the bills again.

"Still interested in those other rooms? So much trouble I'll give you a deal."

"I think I'm fine for now."

Luke walked to the arch between the kitchen and living room. Then he gave a price even lower than the one that Uriel and Carlos gave. "Can get it first thing next week."

"I thought you were firing them."

"I'd probably keep Carlos. If he wants."

I didn't say.

"Well, think on it. I appreciate the business." He reached out his hand and we shook. Walking away, he stopped. "Don't forget that I got that housekeeper from the church. Help you out cheap."

WHY KIKI WAS
LATE FOR LUNCH

I had to stop at the Shamrock on the corner of Las Americas and this woman comes up to me while I'm putting in gas and says can I give her a ride to pick up her check. I say no, no I can't. What does it mean if she's telling me she wants to pick up a check? Who would care, who should? A check isn't an appointment with a hospital or court or picking up a daughter or son at school, not even a lost doggie. She's kind of pacing nervous around there, and I can't tell if she's waiting for someone or a cab, though not a bus, because there's no bus stop here. Then I thought I should take her, because I realized I'd been too mean to somebody too fast. So I call her over and say where do you have to go. Only to Copia, she tells me, and I tell her to go ahead and come on. I'm thinking I will drop her off at the exit and I even tell her I'm going to have to drop you off right there on Copia so I can get right back onto I-10 because I'm in a hurry to get over to the westside. Her name is Iris. I don't think she really cared what I said but like it or not it was all I was going to do. I'm not sure how comfortable I will be with her in my car but she is the one quickly talking about what a beautiful day it is—I guess it was and with the windows down, the air feels fresh and cool—and she's saying how her family never noticed anything like this, they are so selfish and care about themselves and not really even about each other enough. She gave an example of a cook-out on Saturday and the fight that

her brother-in-law got in with their cousin because he is dating some ex-girlfriend, which got her sister mad, too. She is
living in Odessa now and was here just for a few days because
of their dad having cancer and also because she's so homesick,
especially for some tamales from Rosie's. I told her that, yeah,
of course I'd eaten tamales from there, everybody loves those.
Iris liked them best during Christmas and she tells me her
mom and her aunts, when they make them, they think theirs
are so much better. When she asks I say, yeah, I do go to Kiki's
across the street, too, a lot, to be honest. I like to go there and
not only because that's my nickname, too. She really went on
like I maybe owned the restaurant and wasn't telling her. I
tell her would I be driving this if I owned it? She thought I
was funny but when could I be if she hadn't stopped talking?

I don't know why I expected her to be walking south
on Copia after I dropped her off, so that could have erased
my thinking while I was driving north, where she told me she
needed to find Angel to get her check. As we were driving
she was looking for him with her head and arms and hands
and neck and her whole body and a couple of times she was
telling me to slow down more. It didn't seem like she knew
the place where she was picking up her check and so I asked
the name of it so that I could try to find it, too. She says she's
looking for Angel and he should be around here because he
usually is and she says turn left, try this way, and we aren't
even on Copia anymore. I don't understand why she doesn't
know where they are meeting but since I've gone this far
with her I don't know what I am supposed to do otherwise
now and then she says she sees him, there he is, and he's
that mailman in the blue-gray uniform with shorts and the

leather bag and I pull over and before I can say anything, she says she'll be right back and rushes across the street to the sidewalk where he was walking but stops once he sees her. I can't really do anything but wait. You know how I don't even have a radio either, and so with the windows down I try to listen but I can't make out anything, only see that Angel isn't making her happy, isn't giving her a check. It's that he thinks it's probably with Flaco and she has to find Flaco because she doesn't want him to put it in Mario's box first, which would really mess her up, and now we are looking for Flaco, who is also a mailman. I don't really know what else to say as we are driving around looking for this Flaco. I don't want to be ungenerous to her and because she is so sure he is just a few blocks over there I don't say anything. She's squirming around and is almost with her head out the window. She's sniffing and not for a second talking to me now until she sits back and looks over at me and disappointed says what a crazy day, you'd think it wouldn't be this hard. I feel a little sad for her and can't think of what to say to stop, so I just take the turns as she says, thinking we won't find him and then I will just take her back to Copia, when she sees him, there he is there he is. And it is Flaco in a uniform, too, though he also has a hat, and we pull up alongside him walking and she gets out and gets to talking to him, when I lean across the seat and interrupt and say I'm going on now, okay, Iris? She leans into the passenger's window, weeping, Flaco staring at me as though I were causing this. I think she is happy. I think so. Bye, she lets out, nodding. I do a U-turn as she is walking and talking with him, wiping tears, and she waves at me as I pass them.

BLESSING

It was Angie's baby sister who got me to want to play it out again. Little sister was dating my cousin and he told me about Angie's big expensive house and the new dude—an old guy—she married. I got his last name and I made the drive up to Albuquerque and I found the address in the phone book and I got a street map and picked up a six of classy Mexican beer and cruised the west side of the river—which never seems like the same Rio Grande that we see at home—and when I got there, I had to drive the neighborhood slow to find the address but also because my brain kept comparing it all to where she grew up. Which was a two-bedroom house on Alta that was her grandparents'. Her *guelita* still stayed in one of the bedrooms, and her mom—her dad died when she was too young—used the other. Angie and her sister slept in beds on a remodeled back porch, which leaked from above and sagged onto the desert backyard. After they hung up all their pretty dresses on a lead pipe that fit across one wall and the other, there was no other space except for the dresser she had to share with her baby sister and the vinegaroons and scorpions and sometimes red ants that crawled up, ignoring the carpet remnant, through the cracks in the squeaky floors. Her older brother got to fix up a section of the garage. She thought of me as the rich boy because my mom's new man wore a suit and tie. I thought so, too. We'd moved into a big house on Wheeling with the greenest grass on one of the only streets in El Paso where almost all the people on it watered their lawn. I'd been driving, thinking and thinking about us, me and Angie, how time was passing, how we're all supposed to change—you know how that goes. I never saw El Paso as so poor, and maybe that wasn't the word, but you'd have to think something like it driving in this Albuquerque neighborhood, even if I didn't like tract housing and really hated these adobe stuccos. I worked this kind of housing project a lot, though only when I had to. You got shit pay for the work, lots of *mexicanos* working because they'd work for *un kilo de tortillas,* or it'd be with white boys who listened to Van Halen too loud and too much.

The colored strobe lights from behind seemed to hit at the same time as the bump of the siren. I'd been like bear hugging the steering wheel, chugging along almost first-gear slow, even though I was in second, deep into my own head, almost dreaming. I got woked up. I pulled over but did not get out and in the side mirror watched a uniform walk up tight along my side of the truck, his hand near his *pistola.* He asked me for the usual documents. He had the usual shades off.

"So what's going on, Officer?" I asked him.

Another cruiser had come up behind his and its patrol-man had taken a position on the other side of my pickup. This one faced my window now, first eyeing my possessions inside, then digging through some. I hadn't opened a bottle, but there were a couple of empty cans and a lot of paper and nails and a few screwdrivers, a pair of snips and some fast-food napkins, and a few rolls of toilet paper I'd forgotten to take into my apartment. Seemed to me like that's what he stared at the longest.

"It's the plates, right?" I asked. "You guys don't like us Texas drivers, right?"

"So what's your business here?" He handed me a roll of TP.

"I'm looking for my girl," I said. "High school sweetheart, you know?"

"A girlfriend?" He didn't believe me.

"Yes, sir, that's it." I almost corrected him.

He was staring at me still, like I was lying.

"Maybe I look gay. I'm not though."

He didn't break into any smile. "Aren't you driving a little slow?"

"I'm kind of looking for her address. Hard to see them, kind of."

"Because you don't know where your girlfriend lives?"

"Yes and no," I said. I was willing to explain if he'd let me.

"There are numbers painted on the curbs."

"Well, yeah."

"What's her address?"

I showed him. I'd ripped the page out of the phone book. It was circled and underlined.

"That's real nice," he told me, "especially for the next person who can't find this page."

"Sorry," I said.

"You don't know where your girlfriend lives?"

"It's an old girlfriend, Officer," I started. He cut me off again.

"This isn't even the street you're on."

"If I got it right, it's another two streets and then to the left."

He took a few seconds to study me and the toilet paper in the back. "You say she lives at the address you have here?"

"What else would I be doing with it?" I was shaking my head this time, which I shouldn't have.

He did the opposite of shake his head. He put the shades back on and stood there so the sun was in both lenses. "Let's find out if this girlfriend wants to see you."

"Ex," I mumbled, though he didn't give a shit.

We all rolled forward until I stopped, up alongside the curb in front of an adobe style stucco, one cruiser behind me, the other parking in the wide, clean driveway. My officer took off his dark glasses again as he got out, his window down, the police radio up loud. I got out, forgetting the six-pack.

"Stay by your truck," he barked.

I leaned against the door.

An older man in shorts and loafers and a way-too-colorful Hawaiian shirt came through a side gate before either of us took too many steps forward or backward. "Yes?" he asked.

"Do you know that man?" the officer asked him about me.

"I don't know *him*." I spoke first to be heard.

"No, I do not," he said. "Never seen him before."

"He says his girlfriend lives here," the officer told him.

"I said an ex-girlfriend," I told them both.

"Shut up!" the officer said to me.

"My wife and I live here," he said.

"I came to see Angie González," I said, taking a chance.

That got the old guy's attention and stopped the cop. "What is it you want?" he asked me.

"I grew up with Angie," I said. "In El Paso."

Her husband seemed pissed off by this, but he knew I wasn't lying and the police officer saw that, too, and nodded at the other one still sitting in his vehicle. "We've had some robberies around here," he told her husband.

"I just got in town," I said, not directly to either of them. Her husband already didn't like me.

That's when Angie came through the front door and through a patio tunneled with vines of bougainvillea. She was all legs in her shorts and all . . . well, it was an especially pretty white blouse on her. *La morenita* Angie was grown up, a full-out woman now. She didn't recognize me. Her husband gave her a kind of look that was between them. The officer waited for one from her, too.

"Hey Angie," I said. "I got cold ones in this truck."

It took her three seconds. "Oh my God!" she said like she used to in high school.

In his head, her husband was no doubt using the same words as she did. He turned and was back through the side gate, not saying nothing else to her or me, the sockless tennies he wore squeaking behind him like they were scary.

"Sorry," I told her.

"It's nothing," she said.

"Not the best impression, huh? The SWAT team has to come and surround *el rancho* because some dirty Mexican is sniffing around the man's *ruca*."

She smelled good. I knew I could use a shower.

"It's not you."

"So he's, like, an asshole? Or just seems that way?"

I swear she wanted to smile, but she wouldn't. She still had an accent like she hardly knew English, when in fact she hardly knew Spanish. Made me happy to hear it.

I handed her a roll of the toilet paper like it was a prom corsage.

Inside the house it was about as real as one in a TV show. Unmushed sofa pillows poofed up in each of their corners, carpet so vacuumed it had those grass lines you see on football fields, windows still chirping they were so clean, kitchen tiles wet from a skylight. Suddenly I was conscious of me—the hair a little too untrimmed, the old T-shirt a little faded, the black pants a little too gray in the knees and butt, and I even had cowboy boots on. Didn't seem like boots were right. And I brought beer. She used to drink beer. I took off my cheap green *gorra*. It said *Garcia*. I found out it was a fishing reel company, but I liked it for having *Garcia* on it.

We sat on stools, quiet.

"Beer's okay?"

"Of course!"

I handed her one after I twisted the cap. "Not bad," I said. "Nice house, really really nice."

She drank beer to prove something to me, I swear.

"Is he an asshole? Is that it?"

She slugged me in the arm. "His name is Don."

"Don?" I asked. "Not Dionisio? "

"He goes by Don."

"Dionisio comes out Don? Whatever, they're both old, from way back in ancient history."

She slugged me again.

"I mean, as names . . . just, you know, *don* Don . . ." I was laughing, she wasn't. "Okay, I know he's your man, I'm sorry. I'm the asshole."

"My asshole."

I heard that *my* and it spilled all over me. Made the room look crazy. We were smiling at each other.

"It's been so long," she said quietly. "You're more handsome now."

She looked so great I was sucking back drools.

"Lotta good my looks did me."

"You know they did some good."

"So?" I asked.

"So what?"

It was like before, like we still knew some secret about each other. "What about you having a baby?" She didn't even notice that I knew about this like I knew where she lived.

"Oh yes!"

"I can't believe you used the name Brisa." It was the name she told me once would be the name of our daughter.

"Why not? It's a beautiful name," she said.

"I guess *el don* liked it, too, then."

She shook her head. "She's sleeping right now." She started getting more distracted. Then, "You're staying for dinner."

"Hell yeah," I said. "But it's okay? With him?"

She was elsewhere. I dropped it.

"I bet she's beautiful." I opened another beer. "I can't believe you're a mom." I wanted to be Daddy. "I was so lucky back then, nothing else."

She slugged me on the arm hard and grimaced doing it.

"Harder," I told her.

"You've changed so much." Sarcasm that was happy. "Let me go see. . . ." She made eyes and walked out of the kitchen.

She was back alone.

"Is he an asshole? What's going on?" I really was asking now, curious. I wanted to know if she was goofing around.

She didn't defend him. She didn't say nothing.

It made me sad for the dude, kind of. I was poor, dirty, and unemployed. She missed me? Cool. It seemed weird, too. "You struck gold, Angie."

"It's surface. Things don't mean that much."

I looked at her like, if it were there, I'd know. I got shit.

"I think about you," I told her. "But from back home, back then."

She didn't look at me. "Your family?" she asked. "How's your mom?"

"She's okay, you know. She still lives all alone in the house on Wheeling. Everything in there is the same, only a bunch of years later."

"Right," Angie said. "I know."

"How do you know?"

"When I go back, I drive by."

"Really?"

"Really. Seeing if you're there, too."

"Really?"

"Listen, I have to make us dinner," she told me.

She used a food processor. I'd never seen one work before. To get a closer look, I brushed against her. Then I had to ask.

"I don't know why," she whispered to me.

★   ★   ★

For grace, she made me hold her hand. I didn't have to hold his, because he was sitting so far away opposite me, but she did, with her other hand.

Bless us O Lord these your gifts which we are about to receive from your bounty through Christ, our Lord.

I really shut my eyes. I didn't feel just a hand. The words were sounds I heard way back there in some darkness, way back there in a different, slow time. Touching her skin, on her hand even, aroused me like reaching into her bra. I know I wasn't praying right, I knew that. It was wrong.

I was hungry, and I ate, but it was impossible for me to concentrate. He didn't say much. I felt like I shouldn't be there, it was me causing the silence, but I didn't know what else to do. She didn't say much either. It was one of those long, and I mean really long, meals.

"Yeah, I guess I am," I said. I'd caught the tail end of what he was asking and jumped at it. "I do get up early, you're right." I could almost yawn if I let myself. Mostly I was buzzed, really more weirded out, but like a downer-upper mix.

She started picking up the dishes, and I stood to help, but he wanted it all, insisted. She led me to the guest bedroom.

"I'll come by later," she whispered. "Late."

"Angie," I started.

"He takes pills to sleep. Don't worry."

Nothing electrical was plugged in, but it was kind of black-and-white TV in the room. I could watch her like a porn movie. My hand, not real on her hips, not real on her waist. I couldn't stop running hands on that skin so creamy moist it was lotion. When she was on top of me, arching back, holding the baby against her naked chest so the baby could sleep, her hips locked into her eyes. That was the most sick pleasure moment I'd come close to even imagining, all of it like an addict's rush—dangerous, bad news.

"I love you so much," she said after, pressing against me. The baby was sound asleep beside her.

It didn't sound right. It couldn't be anything close to true. No, it wasn't true.

"I can't believe this," I said. I had to get up.

"Baby," she said, "do you still love me?"

I opened a window and went to the bathroom and I came back to the bed. "I don't know what to do now. Maybe I better take off."

"No. It's all right. Please."

My face fell back on the brand-new pillow and fine linen sheets. It wasn't all right to me. It wasn't all right. But there I was. "She's gonna wake up," I said. "She's gonna see me here."

"She's a baby," said Angie.

"Angie, that's what I'm saying."

"It'll be all right. I'm her mother. She knows she's safe."

It was still early, barely eight, when I got up. I had to leave. I tried to sleep once Angie was gone but couldn't. I had to leave. There was no other option. And I would've gone straight out the front door if he hadn't been there.

"Good morning," he said.

"You're up already, too, Mr. . . . ." I didn't mean to talk to him like he was a high school teacher or whatever. It just popped out of me. I was too sleepy, and bumping into him made me jumpy and more nervous.

"Don."

"*Oralé*. Don. Thanks."

"You sleep well?"

"*¿Cómo no?* You have such a beautiful home. Perfect room. Great bed. . . . I'm just used to getting up early."

"Me, too."

I was still stumbling in my head, not yet sure what to say or do.

"You're used to it because of your work."

"Exactly," I said. "Earlier than this. I slept in. Since I'm not working here yet."

"You hungry?" He stood up, set down reading glasses he was using for the newspaper, this morning the rubber *chanclas* slapping his bare heels when he walked. "I have some coffee made."

"No, I'll be fine. I can get something."

"It's not a problem for me. Eggs, cereal, toast. We have options."

"Really nice, *pero no gracias,* really."

"You drink coffee, though?"

He had a mug out already, and he had the carafe aimed to pour. I nodded, no choice.

"Milk here, sugar there," he said, pointing. "Angela sleeps later because of Brisa."

I didn't want to, but I sat down at the table. One of what they called rustic Mexican. I worked with a guy in El Paso who started a business selling this. I wondered what they paid for this one here in New Mexico. "Lot of work having a baby, I guess."

"I try to help," he said, "but she takes the worst of it."

"A lot of work I can only imagine."

"Are you planning to stay? If you need the room while you're looking, I'm sure we can accommodate you."

"Cool, cool of you." But I didn't want to talk about that. Wanted to talk about anything else. There was a bag on the table and inside were blue tortilla chips, and I pulled them to me. "Man, I've heard of these, but I'd never seen them before."

"They're good. I don't know what alignment of stars made me want them for breakfast. Not usual for me."

"Yeah, blue chips for breakfast. Kind of living freaky, Don."

"Funny, yeah, chips with your coffee being wild. I'm a yogurt-in-the-morning kind of guy."

"There it is."

"Try one. They're good, then you'll see. I woke up this morning, and I wanted them. Not like me."

"One of those mornings," I said. I ate one. They tasted like tortilla chips, and I didn't taste any of the blue.

The phone rang. He answered it and talked standing for a minute and then he stopped.

"I have to take this in there, excuse me."

I was eating the chips and sipping coffee I didn't want and now once he was out of the kitchen, I got a rush that said *now*. I wasn't working with a tick tick but since he was taking a while, suddenly, like that, in a sprint I made it out the front door and to my car.

It was near the river, close to downtown, when I realized I had the bag of blue tortilla chips with me, too. Still no idea where I was going, now I was concentrating on them, how I wasn't even conscious of taking them, how it meant worse about me, and for Angie, than me leaving without a word. Don would say I was a rude chip thief—and what would she say, what could she say? I went on eating them, and then I needed something to wash them down. I pulled into a Circle K and bought a tallboy. A dude I couldn't help but notice going in I noticed more coming out. Or he was more into me because now I had a brown bag he recognized. He had long black hair like an Indian, but the rest of him looked like street and homeless. Almost homeless, because his running shoes seemed pretty plush, almost washed white.

"I got no money, boss," I said. He was right outside the door, that look, and he followed me. He didn't move like a homeless dude.

"Just a couple bucks, man. For some food."

He was right behind me as I was opening the car door and shaking my head really or not. "You're hungry?"

"Really hungry, yeah."

I got the bag of chips. "Have these, then. They're blue, but they're really good."

He stared at the chips bag while I started the car.

"Thirsty, too, man," he said, close to the window. "You know?"

"There it is," I said. "Like I thought."

"You know how it is," he said. "Come on."

I shook my head. "You come on. I did my deed. Chips are it."

I was expecting some stupid *pedo,* but he stood up like a man and let it go. I backed out, and when I shifted to drive, I saw him crunching a chip and motioning thanks. I stopped. I waved him over and, like a *don* Don, took the smallest bill in my wallet, a ten, and gave it to him. "Spend it wisely, *compa,*" I said. "Be good."

Sipping the tallboy, I cruised Central trying to decide what to do besides taking I-25 South back to El Paso. When I saw the Frontier Restaurant, I remembered the bowls of green chile they had there. I wasn't not hungry. I didn't know what was wrong with me—besides the nasty Angie sex . . . and all that twisted-up shit I guess I couldn't take. I went in and ordered and found a booth by the window. Albuquerque was like supercool big city compared to El Paso. Even in the morning, there were all these tattooed people and real cowboy types, beside ones only styling it, hippie students with science books, and nerd girls tapping computer keys, and stoner musicians and artists, a couple of them pretty hot, drawing by themselves while they drank coffee. Normal people, too. Then there were the tall and short, light and dark, dumb and smart, fat and bony walking or riding by on bikes, and one cute as a billboard poster. I liked it. A lot. Made me feel like, no matter, I did right even if I did everything wrong.

Even though they called my number, my green chile wasn't up there when I went, so probably I was gone longer than usual, which was why these two dudes took my booth.

"I was sitting there, you guys," I said.

They looked at me, then at each other.

"Sorry," I said.

"It was empty here," one of them said.

"That's because I got up to get my order."

"Let's find another table, Timmy," said the other, starting to slide out.

"Why? Let him find one."

"Why don't you just listen to your friend, Timmy." It's true I said his name with a little disrespect, like it belonged to a five-year-old.

"Fuck you," he said. He was coming out of the booth.

"No," I said, half setting, half throwing my bowl on the table, "fuck you."

I gave him a shove when he was standing there too close, both of us about to throw *chingazos,* when a big man dressed like a cook appeared, stepping between us.

"Take it out of here, both of you!" he said.

Timmy's friend was nudging him away. I didn't want to go.

"Sir," the man said. "Please."

"I just wanna eat my breakfast," I said.

"I'd appreciate it if you'd leave and we don't argue," he said.

"I wasn't doing nothing. I'm not now." I scooted into the booth and started wiping the spilled green chile with paper napkins. Most of it was out of the bowl.

"Sir, I insist you leave."

I didn't say anything. He went away, and when I finally looked over the other way, out the window, I saw that Indian dude who was at the Circle K. I waved at him to come in.

"*Compa!*" I said, standing up, shaking his hand like we were old friends.

He was acting less sure than me. "Sit down, sit, sit. Hey, you still hungry?"

He didn't say no.

"Stay here, hold the table, I'll get us both a bowl of green chile." There wasn't a line at the register for once, so it went fast. They were all watching me, I could feel that, too.

"It's good food, brother," I said when I got back. "You probably know that." I put the receipt on the table. "We're number seven." I was trying to make it easy. "Can't be better."

He still wasn't saying.

"So, what are you?"

That got his attention, even if he was slow with the words. "Two arms, two legs. One dick. How 'bout you?"

I laughed, he smiled. "Okay, you got me. I'll come clean to you. I got two dicks, so I gotta work double hard."

That busted out a real laugh from him.

"I meant," I said, "what kind of Indian?"

"Mescalero."

"Apache?"

"Mescalero," he said.

"Cool, very cool."

He kind of shook his head at me, disappointed, like I'd become a dork for saying he was cool. "What tribe you from?"

"Good question," I answered. "Depends on who's saying. Lemme see. Messican. *Pocho. Culero. Pinche mamón pendejo.*" I was trying to apologize in my way, but he wasn't getting the jokes. "I'm from El Paso."

"Been there. Better here."

"So, what brings you to Burque?" I asked. Another bad. The dude stank. Probably hadn't bathed in a month. I met him begging at the Circle K. I jumped back in. "I drove up to check out an old girlfriend. I did, too. *Híjole.*"

I thought I had him interested but something else at the entrance—at my back—took his attention. So much that before I could look for myself, he had slid across the seat and was standing up. And then he took off! I didn't know it, but there was an exit door that way, back there. Two Albuquerque cops were quick behind, screaming at him to stop, and the whole restaurant went into a gasp. I got up fast and rushed to the entrance and out and I could see him flying, way out ahead. I might have registered more but then the explosion of sound came at me. "Don't move! Stop! Do not move!" The cop had his gun aimed at me. Two more cruisers squealed up and four more came out of those cars and the one with the aimed gun was telling me to lie on the ground with my arms out. Then two or three were on me, one whose knee was on my neck, another on my legs, and my hands were cuffed. I'm sure I was cussing and making noises but they were yelling like I was assaulting them.

I'd been pulled up and now I was being pushed toward a cruiser. "Can you please tell me what the fuck I'm being arrested for?"

"Shut up."

"Sir, I didn't do nothing."

"Where were you last night?"

"Last night? What're you talking about?"

One of the cruisers tore off out of there but two more came, until they sped off. The two cops stayed with me and one opened the back door of his vehicle. "Get in." He pushed, though he kept a hand on my head. He left the door open. The other cop came. They were listening to the police radio and it seemed my Circle K brother slipped them. I heard it. They wanted him for an armed robbery.

Then the cook was there. "Yeah, he's who I called about. I didn't see his friend when he started the fight."

"I didn't start a fight. We didn't even fight! And he isn't my friend. I just met him."

They stepped away from me and soon the other cop was there. "Toilet paper," he said.

Probably I didn't recognize him without his shades on.

"So, you know this is some kind of mistake!"

"Why do you say that?"

"Because you saw where I was."

"That wasn't last night."

"But that's where I was."

"Earlier. I don't know later. And you weren't with your partner."

"Dude's not my partner. I met him at the Circle K just now, *es todo*. He was begging. I gave him a couple bucks and ran into him here."

"You gotta lot of shit stories." He smiled at his own toilet paper humor.

"Officer, that's not fair, that's not right."

"We'll see. We'll see what your partner says about last night."

"So, this is because you think I was with him last night?"

"So far now, it's disturbing the peace and resisting arrest. See what your partner adds on."

"Come on, I didn't do none of that." I wanted to get out of this, but how? He didn't believe me, and he definitely didn't care. "What is it I gotta do?"

"You were born. Until you die, the rest is on you. I'm just doing my job."

TO DOCUMENT

My girlfriend Jennifer rushed in to tell me—I was studying—that she'd talked to them, meaning *him* of course, the
one we looked away from all the time, the one staring at us
from his driveway, always standing there, a driveway to him
like a beach, only you stood there. Staring. The narc, I called
him. She called him *coolio,* which was kind of fun, but it made
me think *culo,* which was not so fun. My mean sarcasm was
something she never got or heard or listened to because she
was a well-mannered white girl. Worse, I knew she really
did think he was cool in some twisted-up way. I figured that
was because she grew up without any danger, or any crazy,
or any just plain wrong, so anything that wasn't like a family
TV upbringing was not only fascinating but exciting. This
also explained why she was with me.

    "He invited us over," she said, thrilled. "Is that wild?"

    "No," I said.

    "Yes it is!"

    "It isn't, Jennifer."

    "Well, I'm going. You don't want to, you don't have to."

    I'd already put down the book. It was always hard to
study where we lived. Music going all the time, people in
and out. Lots of dogs. Cats to step on or around. Beer, vodka,
tequila. Drugs. Noise noise noise. I was the only one who
kept it down. Vanessa and her mousy girlfriend had one room
and my friend Ef, the other. He sold drugs with his cousin

Richard, who was always in the house, sleeping on the couch. They paid the rent, meaning I didn't, which obviously encouraged me to stay. I was on the good path. Because it didn't pay well, to most I had a shitty job as a clerk at a motel and didn't get enough sleep, but I liked it. Studying was my newborn Christianity, and I read a lot there.

I had to go. It was how it was. She decided, I went along. She helped me. I'd never known anyone like her and she made me feel . . . like life was better. Soon, she said, she'd be leaving El Paso—meaning me, too, or the way I took it, that we'd be leaving together.

It was a few days later, a weekend night. The sky was tuned bright, the starlight above mirrored in the streetlight below, the raw desert in front of us as romantically Western as she saw it. They had a nicer house than we did. Maintained better on the outside anyway, the landscaping free of weeds, the decorative rock making the ocotillos and agaves seem ceramic-pot pretty, the palo verde lacy. The front door we knocked on was freshly carved Mexican wood. The inside was nicer, too, all new paint and furniture, like objects inside a frame. She was Natalie, he was Phil.

"I'm Jennifer," Jennifer said, "but please call me Jen. And this is Nino."

"Nino," Natalie said. "How unique a name."

"Is that short for something?" asked Phil.

I would have said no, but Jennifer thought I was taking too long. "Just Nino. Nino the *niño!*" She laughed, and they laughed, too.

"Around here Phil goes by Felipe," Natalie told me.

"Felipe!" said Jennifer, thrilled as ever with what I found irritating. The man was also shaved bald and wearing a light blue coat with wide lapels and a "hip" shirt—maybe cool in New York. She had on a black party dress. Older, she was still cute, so much that it was hard to see how they could possibly have matched up. We were both wearing jeans, though I washed mine, and Jennifer made me iron both the pants and my white guayabera, which I was glad I had. As usual, she was right. It didn't matter what she wore, she made it classy.

"Are you guys from El Paso?" Phil asked me.

"Nino is," Jennifer answered. "I'm from California first, then I moved to Maryland."

"I'm from Philly," said Phil. "I know, Phil from Philly. I know, I know."

"That doesn't work with Felipe, does it?" Natalie cheerfully said to me.

She was speaking to me because I hadn't said a word yet. I might have, I might not have as quickly as I should have, anyway, but in their living room I'd already gotten distracted. It was a spacious room, long pastel blue sofas and chairs circling a wall of glass—the drapes were pulled to their corners so that the panoramic view of the desert and city lay before. No doubt beautiful. But my eyes wanted to lock on the wall opposite, at a painting as big as most picture windows. Hard for me not to see it when I walked in because it was of a woman—a very attractive one—seated and completely naked, her face aroused. The painting blurry, a strange green and pink, at first I thought only my mind made it seem to be Natalie.

"Wine? Or beer, maybe?" said Phil. "I have gin, bourbon ... I have it all. Name your pleasure."

"I can't believe we forgot to bring a bottle of wine or something!" said Jennifer.

"Yeah," I said, "I should have remembered." I would never have thought of it. "My fault, I'm sorry." I didn't look at her, but I was talking to Jennifer.

"Please," said Phil, "you're our guests."

"Wine, white wine," Jennifer said.

"Me, too," I said.

"You do not seem like a white wine man," he said to me.

"It's fine," I said.

We would eat very soon, but for the moment we all sat.

"Oh!" said Jennifer. "It's you!"

Natalie smiled. "Self-portrait."

"You paint? So do I!"

"It's Modigliani, but more now, more contemporary avant-garde," said Jennifer.

"He is my favorite."

They were hitting it off, talking in little screeches and exclamations. Phil was pleased. I thought he was proud that his woman was so hot and proving it in their living room's portrait. So I was more uneasy still. I didn't really like the wine, either, but it wouldn't have mattered what I was drinking. When suddenly the women were going to the kitchen together, and Phil and I had to be alone, lousy was even worse.

He refilled our drinks. I assured him I really wanted another white wine.

"So what about you, man," he said, being cool. "What do you do?"

"For money?"

"Well, usually."

"Only a crummy job. Nothing. At a motel."

He was smiling. "You have other work? For not money . . ."

I didn't answer quickly.

"You know, like your lady is an artist."

"I'm studying. I read. I like to read."

He chuckled like I made that up.

"For school? A grad school?"

"Yeah, maybe. But no." I didn't like to discuss this part of my life. "What about you?" Turning the subject. "What do you do?"

"Retired military."

"Military," I said. "Retired."

He waited, expecting more. Probably most people would ask quite a bit more. In fact, one detail was that he didn't seem retirement old, even if he did seem older. But I didn't care. I didn't want to ask more.

"A lot of people over at your place," he said finally. "All the time."

"Yeah, it's a zoo."

"Partying a lot."

"Not always. Not Jennifer and me."

"Not everybody lives there, though."

"No."

By now he was getting a little peeved. Like he wished dinner was ready. Like he wished I'd tell him whatever. Or maybe exactly.

"So what is it? How many people live there?"

"Roommates?"

It was like he either wanted to stand up or sit better than he already was.

"It's a three-bedroom," I said. "I have one of the rooms. Me and Jennifer. Then our other two roommates."

He drank his drink. I had barely sipped my second glass of wine. I was sure he would say something else, but then we heard Natalie.

"Nino, Felipe, dinner is servido'd!"

Jennifer was right behind her. "You can't believe how good the food looks and smells," she told me. "I think I'm in love with your wife," she told Phil. This made him feel much better, and that made me feel a little relieved, too.

The dinner was probably great, as excellent and unbelievable as Jennifer and Phil gushed, but I was too uncomfortable to do much more than pretend as well as I could. I probably didn't really like this food as much as they did. No tiny eater, I thought good was some eggs with chorizo, or rice and beans made right, avocado with lime, salt, and pepper with warm tortillas. Though she tried to act like it was no biggie, I knew it ticked Jennifer off that I was this way, and it didn't make me feel good that it did.

"I had fun, and I really liked her."

"I know."

"And he's so out there."

"Out there like a narc."

"I don't think they'd care. I bet they smoke it."

"Who'd want to smoke it with them?"

"I definitely would with her. I bet she does. I'll find out."

"With him, then."

"It doesn't seem like he would, that's true. I bet he'd be very interesting if he did. "

"You gotta be joking, right?"

She smiled. She wasn't. I didn't for one second believe she'd want to hang out with him—even her, for that matter. Jennifer was just . . . this was how she was.

Not that I would smoke it with either of those people. I wasn't doing any with anyone. I had put that past me. Even Ef didn't smoke like he used to, not like his cousin Richard and Richard's friends. Not that he wasn't into the white powder some, enough. He did the blow. He insisted he was careful about it, and I believed him. Mostly. Efren was my closest, longest *camarada*. We were brothers. I wanted to believe him. The truth was that he'd been getting loose about his business. Was it because of blow? It was like he was getting it too easy, and he was moving it around too fast. Sometimes the house noise seemed like more than noise. Sometimes it sounded like stupid.

These two young guys coming over were proof. One had long scraggly hair that had braids in it that hadn't been unbraided in a year. Tattoos that seemed like a long-sleeve blue shirt from a distance. He needed food. I'd take him for a meth head, but he smiled too much and too calmly. His partner was a pretty blond, proud of the muscled cuts in his pecs and abdomen. In other words, he went shirtless. Only hippie beads. I was there when they were telling Ef that they felt like they were being followed at first, so they drove around until they lost those detectives. Ef sold to them.

"Are you losing your mind?" I told him after.

"I been doing business with them for a while," Ef said. "They've always been good for it."

"I never seen them before."

"You're not always around, *mano*. I'm telling you, they're good for it, and a solid quantity when they . . ."

"Are you joking? They even said they were followed."

"They said they *thought* they were. *Pero* okay, I see what you're getting at."

"Like, if you saw them, if you were a cop, what would you do? You'd see where these stoned *idiotas* go, who they know, like that."

"You got a point, *simón,* yeah. *Pero* . . ."

"But what?"

"Come on, Nino. Lighten up, dude."

"Ay, you are *so* losing it."

"Look, serious, I'm practically done with the shit now. I know what you're saying."

"You're done?"

"*Ya no más, en serio.*"

"I do not want to see their car here again, ever, okay?"

"Yeah, that's cool."

"They're a bust. I'm telling you."

"*Andale,* brother. I got it, I got it."

Jennifer didn't recognize anything as dangerous. She thought it was all an adventure ride. Material, paint strokes, color. Nothing in her life suggested that she was wrong. I never asked her if she'd even gotten a traffic ticket.

"Detectives," I said. "You heard of them?"

"How would anyone know? Aren't they undercover?"

"No. They drive unmarked cars."

"That's what I mean. That they look like cars, so how would he know?"

"They're as unmarked as a seven-foot quarterback, wearing plaid shorts and a camera, in, like, a cruiser painted plain brown."

"You worry too much."

"Right. That's probably it. Let's forget about it."

"It'll pass," she assured me.

After that we got on our way for a picnic in Cloudcroft with our neighbors, who'd invited us. Phil had a silver flask of cognac and we all shivered after taking swallows. Jennifer was very excited because she'd never been, and with the Mescalero reservation nearby—more excited. She and Natalie were still exuberant over each other, and Phil had got creepier since—it was hot in El Paso—they were both displaying much in their low-cut tops. And they did not shy away from the topic that was on his mind.

"You wouldn't like a nude beach?" asked Phil.

"I'm normal. Of course I like to see naked women. It's not that . . . though probably they don't all look so good, and maybe it's best I didn't see that, either."

The women moaned critically.

Phil loved it. "Not all boobs are equal," he explained.

The women moaned.

"Not all penises are equal, either, Felipe," said Natalie. Jennifer said, "*Uuu.*"

"What's yours like, Nino?" Natalie asked.

I was not good at this. Didn't like it ever, less so with these people who did not make me comfortable.

"Come on," she insisted. "You've seen what we girls have, what about you?"

"When'd he see you?" asked Phil, giddy. "What are you guys doing when I'm not watching?"

"Our painting, my darling."

"You are well-endowed," Jennifer told her.

"You're a couple of handfuls yourself, my lovely."

Both of them seemed to be shoving their breasts forward.

"So what about it, Nino?" Natalie kept on.

"You're asking him to take it out?" cried Phil.

"I didn't mean that, but if that's what it takes!"

I didn't offer a word. I didn't move.

"It's big," Jennifer said to break through. "I've seen it up yummy close."

Both Phil and Natalie howled.

I hadn't drunk that much, and I didn't think Jennifer had, but she was drunk already. Clearly the flask was no aperitif for them. "Settle down, boys and girls," I said finally. "We're still getting there."

"He's no fun but probably right," said Jennifer.

"If he promises to show me later." Her hands were so close to her breasts, it was as though they were someone else's moving in for a feel.

Phil was still laughing too hard as the highway curved to the right, and he didn't turn the wheel enough, so the car wandered into the oncoming lane. We all heard car horns as he straightened it out fast.

After a few moments passed, I offered to drive. Phil's eyes were already locked on the rearview mirror. It was the New Mexico State Police, who finally lit it up. When the patrolman got to the window, Phil was perfect, driver's license and insurance already out: He lost his grip on the steering wheel;

he was very wrong to be driving one-handed. He stepped out of the car, and the two talked by the trunk. Then he came back, shaking his head.

"He was a good man," he said.

"You didn't even get a ticket?" I said. I was sure I'd have been given a DWI test, and I only had a couple sips.

"One of those things," he said. "He understood."

I looked at Jennifer to say, *See?* without words, but like Natalie, she hadn't sobered up as Phil had.

"Look, I don't mean to piss on the party, but I feel like we should turn back. Cash out while we're ahead."

"Poop on," Jennifer corrected me. "The expression is *poop on*."

She and Natalie giggled too much again. All was well. I offered to drive. He wouldn't hear of it. A flask—a second one or refilled?—came out again in Las Cruces. By the time we pulled into his driveway, I was the only one not fresh-start happy to be back. All seemed completely forgotten by Natalie and Phil by the time they were pouring a second bottle of red wine, our picnic laid out on the outdoor patio table. Natalie was bombed. Jennifer, either because she didn't know how not to be agreeable or because she was, kept up. Phil, his crude slobber virtually drooling down her cleavage, didn't seem to disturb her, and Natalie, bumping and pressing against me whenever possible, didn't provoke, either. Though it was true I didn't adore the Gucci food, I got up to leave because I was done for the day.

"I'm not ready yet," said Jennifer.

"Stick around, man! There'll be plenty of time to study later," Phil told me, but then looked at them—an inside joke.

Which did the job of irritating me. Pissed me off. Jennifer didn't move to slow me down even a little as I turned away to leave.

"Wait wait wait," Phil said. Then, slowly, "Wait, wait, wait."

I stopped. I was outside his front door.

"Look," he said. He tried to reach his arm around me, but I dodged it. "Look," he said. "Listen." He was drunk, trying to sound like he was just cool. "You shouldn't go. You shouldn't, man." Did he wink? "Look. Nat. You know? You know, man, you know! She likes you."

"Your wife likes me," I said.

"Come on, man. You go with her, you know. She wants that. You'll like her."

I was about to laugh. I had enough time to bounce around what to say. I mean, I might choose to have sex with this man's wife, though not right then, and not interested at all, really—but whatever, it wouldn't be as much for *his* pleasure as mine in fucking him over by doing her.

"I'll take care of Jen," he said.

My ears heard that faster than I did. So did my arms and my hands and my voice. "Fuck you, you asshole!" I straight-armed his chest with both hands, tumbling him into the front door loud and hard.

"What are you doing?" he yelled. "Are you out of your mind?"

As he steadied himself—"Wait a minute, hold on a minute"—it seemed like he was coming toward me aggressively, not backing away. It could have been to reach out kindly. Who knows? I didn't care. I hit him solid—first a left to stun him, and then a right that, I'd have to admit, punished and slammed him.

Both the women were at the open door screaming. I couldn't say if it was at me or about him. His nose and mouth were bleeding. I went home.

And yes, I was mad. No doubt that had something to do with my bad reaction when I walked in and saw those two dopers in the house again. They were standing in the living room when I asked, probably too loud, what they were doing here again.

"I don't have nothing to do with it," Ef said, backpedaling from all of it completely.

"It's me," said Richard. He stood up straight, which he didn't do so often. "I'm the one who told them. It's cool, Nino, honest."

"It is, *vato,*" the blond said to me. He was wearing a torn T-shirt, his beads over that. "We got the message. Seriously, reallys. Like today, just now, we didn't park outside your house. We parked below the arroyo, and we hoofed it up. The little kids thought we were maybe desert aliens. It was cool."

These two walked a half mile through the peaceful family neighborhood, as inconspicuous as two ice-cream trucks. Quickly I traveled beyond mad into controlled and steady. This was finished, it was time to move along. Even before Jennifer came home, I was packing. She was still dealing with what happened next door, which, it was true, seemed to me a less-important past already. She was so furious at me, she said, truly embarrassed by me. Even as she was going on, though, I caught fascination growing in her voice, the thrill of a ride. Here was an adventure she had witnessed and lived through.

The Old West! Her Chicano boyfriend when she lived on the *frontera*! I'd loosened two teeth, not broken his nose, even though it took a while for them to stop the bleeding there. We even started smiling.

"God, I would never be with him," she told me. "I can't believe he even thought it was possible."

"Glad to know it'd be okay if I was with her."

"She is a turn-on," she said, giggling. "Pretty hard to not want to get naked with her."

It had never crossed my mind what she might be thinking. Talking about the colorful incident and about sex-starved Natalie made Jennifer, still a little drunk, affectionate. In bed, whatever I wanted to do was fine with her.

"We got no choice now," I said. "We have to leave. They're out of control."

"We'll go to my place," Jennifer said.

"You mean you still have the apartment?"

"Of course," she said. "Where did you think I did my work? When I slept? Here?"

"I guess I assumed you gave it up once you lived here."

"When you're at work, those crazy hours you get, I'm there. I'm there a lot."

"Here I thought you were at the college."

"I wouldn't get in this bed if you weren't in it."

"Never thought about it once."

"Such a strange man you are. You read too much."

"All the time you could have been with Phil."

"Or Natalie," she said.

We were on our way for the last few boxes two weeks later when, as I was about to turn into the street, I caught sight of the buzzing hive of police cars in front of the house. Phil stood out like a rodeo clown. I was driving slow enough that I could straighten out the turn.

"We'll know in a minute, but I don't think they saw us. I don't think he did, either."

"My camera's still there!"

We headed back to her apartment.

"I can't believe I left it there. I don't want anyone to take it."

"You can get it back if they did."

"I can't believe I left it. I don't know why I brought it last time."

"To document," I reminded her. It'd been the first time I ever heard that phrase used. "Us here, this time and place on the Texas border." I remembered it like a book title.

"I already took most of the pictures I wanted. It's why I forgot it."

At her friend's apartment, we waited on news. I didn't think it was such a good idea for her to call and ask Natalie. After a few hours, I finally reached Ef's sister. Everyone at the house was arrested, at least nine people. It was four ounces of cocaine and a good stash of marijuana. The coke deal was arranged by a friend of a friend of Richard, who was really a narc. What she understood, they had a warrant for me. At the least, it meant I'd be picked up and need to have a lawyer, with all the jail time and expense between. She didn't hear anything about Jennifer's name.

"What?" I asked. She was as upset as I'd ever seen her.

"One time he asked," she said. "And I told him."

"Names?"

"Everybody's. Everybody who lived there. Yours, and mine, too. Last names. It seemed like harmless conversation. That he was curious, the same way I would be."

"That's all you told him, though?"

"Yes," she said. But she wasn't done. She wasn't quick with it, she wasn't done. "I talked too much to Natalie."

"He's not the narc, but he could have called it in."

"Me, too?"

"He was pissed off at me." I was thinking, and she was crying. "But just as likely dealing with those *payasos* Richard let in."

"I'm sorry, I'm really sorry, Nino! I'm scared now."

"We're all right, especially here."

"You think they'll be looking for my car?"

"There won't be an all-points bulletin."

She was on full alert. "They won't know where my apartment is. I never told her about that."

"Jennifer," I said, "*cálmate,* take it easy."

But she couldn't, or she did in another way: She had her girlfriend and the boyfriend of get all her things from the apartment, even the camera from the house—it was still there—and she was gone in three days, driving to California, or Maryland, or somewhere, she couldn't tell me, even as she kissed me good bye. I quit my job at the motel, which is to say I never showed up again, not even to get my last check. I had her apartment free for the next three months, until I got worried by the second angry letter—not from the landlord but from her grandfather, who was still paying the rent but said I would have to leave or else. Or else? He'd stop paying. Her? He didn't say he knew, but he knew I was there, he knew my name to mail the letters. I never heard from Jennifer again.

And so rested the twenty-five-year-old memory of the rich girlfriend way back when I'd never imagined using airports and rental cars. I'd been to Phoenix a few times, but it was already years ago. I didn't like it then and still didn't. Sedate as it was, the hotelish lobby layout seemed hard to follow. Maybe it was why retired types were hired to nice it up to people like me who looked lost. A half hour before takeoff, I was afraid of being late for the flight. The old man in the blue vest at the elevator who came over to me seemed more like a Walmart greeter.

"No," I said. "I'm fine, thanks."

"But what I'm saying . . ."

"It's all right," I said, rushing an escalator. I thought I heard what sounded like my name, but I dismissed it. Since I had frequent-flyer-premium advantages, I got through what would have been a long screening line fast, just in time to hear the explanation that the flight would be delayed for about forty minutes.

Which was okay. I bought a turkey and Swiss sandwich from the *mexicanos* working there, asking if they were miserable in Arizona because of the new law. They both laughed when I said how it wasn't fair that pretty papers covered turkeys and big cheeses so fast and for so little coin. I found a vinyl seat across from the gate, near two East Indian Americans and a man from Dallas who knew one of them: This afternoon flight was always late. Nobody thought there should be weather issues, but there was rain here, wind there. Like almost all, only a few of them women, each had a computer open on their lap, the Dallas man with his Bluetooth earpiece blinking, him talking, typing, both.

Moments before the first-class boarding call, the old man greeter approached. Many people were already standing near the gate.

"Excuse me, sir, but do you have your documents?"

I was not prepared. Some seconds passed, and people sitting around within range both stared and looked away. I stood with my bag.

"You don't remember me?"

I had no choice but to walk toward him to get to the gate.

"Probably better that you don't recognize me," he said.

I'd passed by him, but it wasn't like I could go too far.

"It's Phil," he said from behind me, pausing. "Felipe. Of Felipe and Natalie."

I turned. It could not be the man I knew. He was so old. Overweight, he was fragile, beaten.

"We've been here for years," he said maneuvering closer to me. "She's had cancer. It's been tough, on both of us."

His teeth were from a museum or an archeological dig. I moved to the other edge of the business attired—dress shirts and silk ties, pleated slacks and shined dress shoes that never scuffed, executive leather briefcases—waiting for my time in the line. I was so not interested.

"Nino, are you doing . . . better?" People stared at him, then me. It wasn't true, but it seemed the only conversation. "And Jen? We still think of her. You both."

My group was next. "I didn't mean to make you mad. It's Arizona."

He was pathetic, and I knew others felt bad for him, that I was heartless. I was relieved when I finally handed my boarding pass to the airline attendant, who ran it over the laser beam and thanked me. I was almost in the chute.

"I'm sorry," he said louder so I'd hear.

On an aisle seat, alone still, I was cramped anyway. Was he sorry about Arizona, or possibly about what happened back when in El Paso? I wished I could have upgraded. I rubbed my closed eyes and planned to sleep. I knew I would never see him alive again.

HACIA TEOTITLÁN

The last time Ramiro Areyzaga was in Mexico was so long ago it was more like a fairy tale. That was Coyoacán, which is Mexico City but which isn't anything like it. He was seven years old and had traveled with his mother and his sister and brother, which also made it such a happy memory. A place of lush green shade, both a forest of trees and a jungle of huge waxy palm leaves, and a *zócalo* of marionettes and dancers, musicians and painters, with toys and balloons for the little ones and shawls for his grandparents. And of course the church, like none he'd ever seen since, all the cool stone space, and God—which he never got over, so much so it stayed inside him, quietly, the rest of his life, like it was the word *México* itself. And there were candied apples and cups of fruit for sale everywhere, like *piña, coco, granada,* papaya, mango, guava, and the sweetest juice squeezed from the ugliest oranges. It was his sister who was so afraid of them, because their peels seemed faded and blotchy and had black spots and were small, nothing like they were from the markets at home, where they were polished and bright as plastic. She refused to drink any, so he and his brother loved it even more just to torture her. Though they talked about going back whenever they were together, none of them ever did, and now he was the only one still alive.

What he did first to come back to Mexico was go online. He thought of Coyoacán, and when he looked, it was that there were so many possibilities, there were too many. There was only one ad for a room in Oaxaca, misplaced, it seemed, in the Mexico City listings. It was written in a less-than-perfect Spanish, which he could tell even if he'd lost so much of his own first language. He knew very little about Oaxaca, really—better said, he didn't know anything but the name—so he read a little. What he liked was that the weather was said to be consistent all seasons, ideal, and that was it: decided. He wrote a query and in a few days came a reply. It was a *departamento* owned by a Sra. Noemi Luisa Campos Villegas. She lived with her daughter. It was in her house. It was newly carpeted, with a single bed, a sofa, two chairs, a table, and a lamp. He would be allowed to share her refrigerator and kitchen. It was very nice, she wrote, and, yes, it was still available.

He got into a van from the airport, which filled with workers, men with new and old straw hats, and a young couple. All of them were so short. Ramiro was tall, as Mexicans go, and his legs were so badly confined behind the driver's seat that he had to pull the left one up with his hand so it wouldn't cramp. A younger boy—he was maybe nineteen—was there, too, and asked him where Ramiro was from. The boy was from a pueblo, on the mountain below the ruins of Monte Albán. The pueblo had a name Ramiro couldn't exactly understand, even though he heard the word twice. The boy had been in Santa Maria, California, picking strawberries. There was so much work, he said, and he would be going back in a week. He was proud. The boy would have liked to talk more, but Ramiro didn't. Not to be impolite. It's only that he wanted to be quiet. He started listening to the couple sitting behind him.

Sometimes it did sound like Spanish, but also it didn't, not all the words—even the words that did, didn't really. Soon these other passengers were dropped off and the driver found the address of his rental near Tinoco y Palacios, off Quetzalcoatl. The *taxista* was kind and carried one of his two bags down a rock pathway where they could see numbers. They found it. Ramiro tipped him big with a twenty-peso bill.

Sra. Campos came down her stone steps, greeted him without much emotion, and then led him to a few more steps and opened the padlock for some arched, wrought-iron gates. Then she pushed open a wet, tired wooden door to show what was now his home. It was a basement in every way, with a faint scent of mildew and dust. The carpet was indoor-outdoor, and was probably not old, though it was hard to see it in the darkness. She had turned on the two switches. The small, clear bulbs were maybe 25-watt. She showed him his bedroom, his bathroom. A frayed towel was there for him, and there was a tiny square of soap, wrapped, nameless, from what was probably a hotel. At the small wooden table, with two chairs, where she had also put a bouquet of assorted flowers to welcome him, he counted out the agreed-upon rent money. She smiled to herself like it was a reward. She led him over to the interior stairs that climbed up to another door. That was the entrance to her home and the kitchen he could share. They went in. Her home was spacious, with tile floors and modern furniture, high walls with many picture windows, and even original artwork on her interior white plaster walls. Her daughter, Elda, was there. She was unbashfully excited, as though Ramiro were a new friend. What is your name? Where are you from? What does that look like? What do you do? She was learning French, not English, she told him, but she wanted to learn English, too. Ramiro could see that Sra. Campos wanted Elda to be still, but resisted saying too much these first moments. She apologized, explaining that Elda was eight. Now she told her that she needed to calm down and go to her room, and, pouty lips aside, she disappeared.

The kitchen was modest and cramped, and so was the refrigerator. Sra. Campos made a small space for what he wanted in it. She showed him where there was a Teflon pan for eggs and where he could get a plate. She was very specific, very precise. There was a washing machine and a dryer, and she patiently showed him all the necessary plugs that would need to be unplugged and plugged, then plugged and unplugged, and the hoses that would need to be hooked and unhooked, and so on. These were all opportunities, he knew right then, that would not be good to share with Sra. Campos—better to find a restaurant, a laundry. He thanked her and said good night and found his stairs back down.

There was so much in his life he wasn't sure of anymore. He was tired, he wasn't really tired. Was he hungry? He could be, and he could skip it, too. Mostly skip it. There was still one thing he really planned, and that was walking. He wanted to push himself, walk like never, to drop from that tired if that's how it was to be. And he began, a long way down Tinoco y Palacios until it changed names a few times, and then a long way back up, on the raised sidewalk, a cool night, alongside the buses and cars and taxis and *motos,* all the way down the two-lane street, the doors of both homes and stores closed and locked, dodging here and there the protrusions of wrought iron or cement sill around a window, careful not to step inside a hole or trip on a chipped curb. The night was already so uniquely dark that he wanted to walk with his eyes upward, until he heard what sounded like a parade coming toward him from up the hill. Students had gathered next to Santo Domingo, lighting rocket fireworks that whistled and blasted so loud they set off car alarms, and were joyous about what seemed like marching music led by a tuba—they sang and danced along to many that were their favorite hits. Ramiro sat long after they all left.

Before he finally went back to his new home, he saw a white stand lit up especially bright in the blackest night with virtually no other light competing. While one of the black-haired women made balls of *masa* and pressed them into tortillas, the other, beside a coved iron disk, hot from beneath the red embers at the top of a barrel drum, dropped cheese and spooned a sauce of tomato and folded. There was a TV on a welded rack of the stand—showing a *novela* from Mexico City—and Ramiro sat on one of the plastic white stools beside a family. When he asked what they offered, the younger woman gave more names he didn't know. What goes inside? There were options of cheese or beans or chicken—no *tasajo* this night, no beef—with *yerba santa* or *flor de calabaza*. He pointed to one warming that he had seen her assemble— like that one. He ate her *tlayuda*—what he would've called a quesadilla—as if he were hungry, though calmly and slow, because it was how they all were, even as they talked.

He smacked his head on the low arch that fit around the wrought-iron gate to his new home. He lay down on what was not much of a bed. Maybe the smallest he'd ever tried to sleep on, and a mattress that seemed thinner than a seat cushion. The pillow was even thinner. He finally took out a warm coat and rolled that up for his head. Because the floor of his basement *departamento* had the incline of the hill, the mattress slid whenever he moved. He was determined to stay as patient as one of the *zapotecos* he'd been encountering since he had arrived. And this felt just right, too, wordless spiritual advice. The test was when a dog started barking and whining, sometimes very close, sometimes a little farther away, and though he slept, he slept poorly.

The morning came chilled and there was only a little light drawn in. He scraped his knuckles on the ceiling changing out of an extra sweater he'd put on to keep warm. The ceiling was only an inch above his head, and plywood lines that made little concrete ridges caught one knuckle and it bled. He went into the bathroom. It was small, too, a few inches wider than the commode. The shower, he found, had the same inch or two on either side of his shoulders, as it did in height. He went out, ducking the low arch, out his *pasaje* toward the street, when he was stopped by a small, dark man with a chair outside a store whose name seemed to be only Abarrotes.

"Good morning," he said, standing up slowly, formally in style and intent.

"Good morning," Ramiro said.

"Aren't you the American living in her home?"

"Yes," he said, "in the home of *la señora* Campos."

"How good, how good," he said. "You know, I've been to the United States. Two times."

"Really?"

"Yes. The first time, Fresno, California. The other, Minnesota. The fields. Cold, it was very cold there. I didn't like Minnesota."

"I can imagine."

"My family is from Zimatlán, and it gets cold, but not cold like that. Now I live here."

"A business owner."

"And you?"

"My family started in El Paso, but most of my life in Pico Rivera, Los Angeles."

"How good, Los Angeles. How good."

"Yes and no. It's more beautiful here in your country."

"I have family who have children born in the United States."

"Really?"

"You are not like the tourists who visit. You come to see home."

"Yes and no. I've never seen Oaxaca before now."

"You fit?" He was looking back at the *departamento,* away from the street. "You are large for the space, aren't you? More like an American."

"Seems so. Maybe."

"I have seen it. Good for one my size, but you . . ."

"Ramiro," he offered.

"I'm Benito," he said.

"Like the president."

"Juárez, too, yes."

"That's beautiful."

"I'm here all the time. You can come into my store."

"Very generous. When I need something."

"At your service. You only have to tell me."

"Thank you, Benito."

Ramiro walked until he found a place for coffee on Morelos that he especially liked. It offered everything from *molletes* with beans to bagels with cream cheese and this time, the first time, he ordered a mollete, because he loved French bread, though he really only wanted some coffee. He would read as well as he could the newspaper that was sitting there. And then he would walk in the warming sun until many of the city streets and buildings looked familiar to him because they were like the others.

When he got back that first morning, Sra. Campos was at her car, about to leave.

"Hi, Ramiro!" said Elda, inside, in the back, excited.

"Everything's fine?" Sra. Campos asked. "Do you need anything?"

"Nothing. Well. There is a dog. That barks."

"It's Loli."

"Loli!" cheered Elda. "Mi loo-lii, mi loo-lii. . . ."

"Elda, please! Settle down! Loli only . . . needs to know you . . . that you are living here."

"Then, it's your dog."

"Yes," she said, still upset with her daughter. "She won't bother you," she told him.

"She won't?" he said.

"She only needs to know you, then she will be as always."

It was, in his way of deciding to come here, better that there wasn't much inside the *departamento* to keep him in the mildew must, without much light. By late morning, the bright sun became too warm, and Ramiro learned to walk the sidewalks on the shady side, stepping around the women in the red dresses of the *triquis,* or the *mixtecos,* or *zapotecos* in their bland aprons and long skirts, arms lifting necklaces or *rebozos* or spoons, selling like beggars, or quickly passing with baskets balanced on their heads. Or the men with those narrow-brim, round straw hats, their eyes making the pitch, showing paintings or hammocks or shirts. In the *zócalo,* away from restaurant tables and chairs under the colonnades, Ramiro walked around the laid-out tourist crafts and pottery, around the stands of fresh corn and burgers and fries—*elotes* or *esquites, hamburguesas* and *papas*—and popcorn and *chicharrón,* dodging and bumping women and men and children and cars near the *mercado* with fruit, piles of scissors, toys, or grasshoppers in chile or natural, *nopales,* radishes, flowers of every kind and color. Musicians played the accordion, the violin, the marimba, the guitar. A man pushed a cart of live chickens; another, candies. Away from the church, a demonstration: *¿Por qué los Lopecinos y los Hernández no?* Beside the church, they gathered around a clown this day and around a mime painted silver another. Ramiro was invisible passing the American, French, English, and German students in their shorts, sandals, headsets, and packs.

He found an inexpensive full-menu *comida corrida* for an afternoon meal. He picked at it. If he was hungry later in the evening, he went to the stand for a *tlayuda* or *mamela.* But he began to always stop where one lady sat, a few blocks from the Templo de Santo Domingo. She would sell fruit in a plastic box that in the States would be for a take-out sandwich.

She had much, and at first he'd so often get the *coco con chile y limón,* that that's what she, from then on, said to him first, after she smiled so happy that he came to her again.

"Hello!" she said, and she reached for the box with *coco.* "Coconut with chile and lime, I have it right here for you."

"How good, thank you, but today maybe I will try the papaya."

"Get them both, young man," she said, squeezing lime on the fruit. "You can." She looked at him. "You should."

She was probably not so much older, though any would call her a grandmother, and she could be very old. It was hard for him to know with these *zapotecos.* She'd told him she had been orphaned at seven and worked thirty-eight years at a *puesto* a few blocks away, but once she hurt her leg and couldn't stand all day anymore, a year ago, she started selling her fruit at this corner, closer to where she lived, sitting at this corner.

"Maybe tomorrow," Ramiro said. "Today, only the one." Some days he would buy two, but since he didn't have a re-frigerator, he would throw what would be one away. Since it was only a few pesos, sometimes he bought the unnecessary box just to please her. It was almost as if she were his only friend here.

"How are you today?" he would ask about everyday.

"My body hurts," she said once. "I had to get up at three in the morning."

"That is early," Ramiro told her.

"I had to get water. I had to bathe myself."

"So early?"

"Yes, and the water was cold." She tightened the blue and yellow shawl she had around her. "I am still cold."

"Maybe you should set up on the sunny side," he said.

"But I have to care for the fruit," she explained.

That was a day he bought two, and she gave him a small bag of peanuts with chile on them as a bonus.

When he reached the *pasaje* to his new home, Benito was there to greet him. His store was where he bought his water and toilet paper and sometimes a newspaper to take inside with him to read in the yellow lamplight at the table.

"How are you, Ramiro?" Benito would say, standing up from his chair. "How was your day?"

"All fine," he would tell him. "Thank you so much."

"How good, how good."

There had been one bad day. For some reason, he couldn't open the padlock at his gate. He was tired because he'd walked for so many hours that hot day. His feet hurt and his legs ached. He needed to go to the bathroom. He was sweaty, and it was becoming as dark out as it would be there inside. He felt unnaturally confused, could almost convince himself that the key had been changed somehow, or it wasn't maybe the same lock. Like time itself was off and wrong. He had stopped taking that pill weeks before he'd gotten here. He'd been told that this could be how it would come at him, that it would get harder and harder, he would tire, and he would want only to sleep very deeply. Not knowing what else to do, he went for Benito, who came back there with him.

"I'm afraid I'll break the key," Ramiro told him.

"It's dry, the lock," Benito said when it clicked. "I'll spray some oil in it."

"Thank you, Benito. Thank you so much. I'm sorry I had to bother you."

"Are you all right?" he asked.

"I think so, yes."

"I don't think so," he said. "In there, it doesn't fit you."

So much had improved since then, though. Just as he would learn to sit down when he was changing his shirt to not bang his knuckles on the ceiling, he adapted to his home in other ways. His eyes, with the light of his memory, began to see more and more in an amp of bulbs no stronger than candles, and he showered with an especially careful calisthenics for washing his feet or hair. At first it was only the newspaper he bought to read at the table. But in a dimmest corner, where he couldn't help but finally look, on a limb of storage shelves, he had dusted off old, oversize books, weathered and smelling, too, with fortified bindings stamped and gilded, built like trunks shipping out for a king or queen. There was a 1940's atlas, with both topographical and political maps, even with streets and monuments of certain cities in Europe, North and South America, and an ornately typeset *La Historia de México: Conquista y Revolución*, and several odd-lettered volumes of an encyclopedia of science. Best of all were several photo albums: the oldest photos, golden and gray, professional and from a studio, certainly of Sra. Campos's family, all set on pages with gummed corner holders; the newer, Kodak black-and-whites, of more recent years, many with deckle edges, of her as a baby, as a child Elda's age, and then as a serious-minded teenager, and then with the young man who she probably had married and then moved with here to Coyoacán until . . . their lives changed somehow, why Ramiro would never know, because he only waved hello and goodbye and paid another rent.

The barking had ceased after only a couple of days. He had learned that whenever it became time for Sra. Campos and Elda to go to sleep, their retriever was put outside. And Loli came right to his bathroom window and slept against it because there was a smoothed, rock surface, not dirt, for her to lie on. And it was true that she cried when she heard him, but it had become a whimper for him to open that window. "Loli, Loli, Loli," he would sing. She would wiggle, squirm, and squeal about seeing him, pushing her head between the wrought-iron bars, sniffing his hair, trying to learn whatever he'd done wherever, while he patted and cuddled her head and snout. Unless the night was too cold, he left it open for her to see him on the bed and so he could see her, too. And many times in the middle of the night, after the bed had slid too far and he had to get up to push it back, he would say her name, Loli, so that she would whine just a little for him—and this would even help him sleep.

"Good morning," Benito said, standing from his chair. He did have customers, even if Ramiro never saw any himself. "How'd you sleep?"

"Good, thank you."

"How good, how good," he said. He looked at Ramiro like he wanted to say more.

The air was clean, the sky as blue as a painted wall. Much time had passed and he felt fine. Like he was fine. Like he was even better. Which, as he understood it, wasn't supposed to happen. So before he stopped for coffee, out of curiosity, he visited a pharmacy. It wasn't that he wanted it. He was not going to take it anymore, ever. He only wondered if. He waited by the glass cases for one of the women in the white smocks, and when it was his turn, he gave her the name of the drug. She looked it up. No, she told him, it was not available. No, she had never heard of it. Possibly he had the name incorrect. She even offered to let him look through the pages of their book.

And so he walked on. He stopped for coffee, *pan tostado,* and he read the daily news. He felt he was getting better at that, too. It was a Sunday. He left the café, and, as always, he walked to get tired. He walked east past the Periférico, the boulevard that circled the city, and then, when it ran out of sidewalk and just about street, he turned back. A little tired, he was glad to rest at a light at the Periférico, where a bus was also stopped. He decided to get on. He stepped up the bus stairs, not sure where exactly it would be going, but this pleased him, too. The driver told him he'd collect later. And so he drove. Most of the bus curtains were closed, so it was hard to see out, though they were traveling east, the northern mountains alongside the road. Few talked, though those who did were quiet about it. It filled with more small, dark men carrying day bags and straw hats, and small, dark women with pink nylon shopping bags and shawls and little kids, smiling, curious about everyone. When the conductor came for the money, Ramiro didn't know where his stop was. The man laughed like Ramiro only got the name wrong and said he owed six pesos. When he decided to get off where many others were, both the conductor and the driver shook their head no. The crossing he wanted was ahead, each assured him. And when they got there, they told him, and he got out. It was a concrete overpass and a road leading north toward the mountains. He started walking until a taxi stopped him. It was full of a family—two children, a grandmother, a grandfather, a young mother—but the young driver made room for him in the front passenger's side. He had stylish hair, pomaded so it was wild in all directions on the top.

"Five pesos," he told him.

"Does it come with beans and tortilla for dinner?" Ramiro asked.

They all laughed. "If you want," the driver said, "we can serve you black beans, not the brown ones you eat up there, and my family can make you much more."

From the backseat, they all smiled and agreed.

"We have good food, honest," the driver said. "But you probably came for the blankets."

"Blankets?"

"It's why everyone comes here."

"Here?"

"Teotitlán."

"I didn't know," Ramiro told him. "I was on the bus, and then I got off. I thought I was in California."

They all laughed. It made them all happy, like they would tell the story later.

They drove up the road and wound around some well-made village streets and then he stopped.

"Here it is," the driver said. "But if you want to eat . . ."

Ramiro wanted to, but that seemed like too much. "Maybe later?" he said. "Where do I go?"

"It's only a few blocks up."

"What's your name?"

"Francisco," he said. "Frankie, in English. I was in California."

Ramiro told him his name and thanked him.

"Ask for me," he said, "if you need a ride back, or if you want to stay."

It was going dark. He passed a couple booths still open for their dyed and woven blankets and almost passed under the high entrance gate of the churchyard, hesitated, and instead went on where he saw people. It was a basketball game, full court, on what might have been the razed and cleaned foundation floor of an ancient, large building. Each team had modern uniforms, and there was a referee in stripes with a whistle, and the few people along the sides cheered, not loud, when a basket was finally made. Church bells began ringing. He looked behind and saw a young man pulling the rope from the backside of one of the towers. In the sky over the church was the moon in crescent, with two stars hung beneath it, and the sun, setting, was decorating the sky like it was one of their blankets.

Instead of attending the evening church service, he walked until he found what was a restaurant. He took one of the plastic chairs and ordered a water as it became fully dark. He asked the owner if he knew the taxi driver Francisco, which of course he did, because everybody knew everybody. The owner flagged down a little *moto,* an enclosed three-wheeler with two seats in the back, and they bounced through rutted and dug-up dirt streets. He stopped behind Francisco's taxi. He was chewing, holding a half-eaten tortilla as he came out of the brick house.

"We already finished dinner," he told Ramiro. "We already ate all the beans."

"If you drive me back, we can stop and I'll buy you a hamburger downtown."

"Downtown Oaxaca? That's a lot of pesos, *güey*."

"That's good, right?"

"I'll take you," he said.

Ramiro got in the back; Francisco's wife got in the passenger's side. She was maybe a year younger than him, eighteen at most. He took a couple of full, cloth-covered buckets of *masa*. Francisco drove slow on a dirt road so ungraded it was impossible to talk, a road that followed along open fields of chopped-down corn and nothing else, which eventually set them aside rock and mud walls too high to see above, through more fields and into another pueblo, where the road leveled. It was his aunt's, where he parked to drop off the buckets to her. There was a double-hinged metal gate wide enough for two cars, and a crowd of children held one open. A black and white mutt had approached, barking.

"Don't be nice to that dog," one of them told Ramiro. "He is a dirty, bad dog."

Even the dog seemed to understand, and squirmed both with fear and for forgiveness.

"He only wants love," Ramiro told the children. "Don't you?" The dog wagged but was afraid to get too close.

They all laughed. "That is a bad, dirty dog," the same bigger girl said. The smaller ones laughed more.

"I live with a bad, barking dog, too," Ramiro told them. "My Loli also gets too dirty."

"Loli!" a couple of them repeated, and they laughed.

"No," the big girl said, serious. "*He* is a bad dog."

Francisco came back, and they took off. The highway to Oaxaca wasn't much farther ahead, and they were soon on it.

"I didn't like it there," Francisco told him. "I never liked it."

"Where in California?"

"Moorpark."

"I know where it is," said Ramiro. "You were working?"

"I was learning English," he said. "I couldn't."

"In school?"

"High school. Two years. I never liked it. I couldn't learn."

"You just didn't want to be there," said Ramiro. "Sometimes you just want . . ."

"It's hard to learn another language," said his wife.

"Sure it is," Ramiro said. "Did you grow up speaking Zapotec?"

She said a word that he guessed was *yes* in the language.

"Yes," Francisco said. "That's what she said."

She laughed and Ramiro laughed.

"Tell me a word," Ramiro said.

"What?" she said.

"*¿Cómo estás?*"

"*Shai yu,*" she said.

"Shy you," he said back. He said it like it was in English. She was very pleased, smiling big. "Yes," she told him.

"I will remember," he promised. "It's like two words in English."

They all laughed.

"The answer is *bwen,*" said Francisco, seeing him through the rearview. "It means *bien.*"

"Ben," said Ramiro. "It's like the Spanish."

"No," said his wife. "*Bwen*."

"Ben," Ramiro said again.

"*Bwen*," she said again.

"Ba when," he said.

She really thought he was hilarious.

"Shy you," said Ramiro. "Ba wen . . . *Bwen*."

"Yes!" she told him.

"I think I want to learn more, but I'm afraid I can only learn a couple of words at a time."

"I know," said Francisco. "And when you learn a new gringo word, you forget one you thought you had."

They all three laughed.

"In other villages, they have even more, other words," said Francisco's wife. "Like, *wenka*."

"*Wenka*," said Ramiro.

"Yes!" she said.

"It means *fine,* too," said Francisco, practicing his English.

"But in another village," said his wife.

"How are you?" said Ramiro. "*Bwen, wenka, shai yu.*"

She thought that especially funny.

"*Fine, fine, fine,*" said Francisco.

They dropped Ramiro off near the *zócalo*.

"*Shai yu,*" Ramiro said instead of good-bye.

"*Wenka,* good," said Francisco. "I have two other languages, too."

He didn't live that far up the hill. He felt strong walking. He would even say he felt good. Or that if he still didn't care anymore, this was happiness, living on, not ending.

Benito stood from his chair outside Abarrotes as Ramiro approached. There were no customers, but it seemed he was there from morning to night. "How was the evening?" he asked.

"Good," Ramiro said. "*Shai yu?*"

Benito would never stare, but it meant the same looking away.

Ramiro couldn't tell if Benito understood or didn't or if he said it wrong, but everything between them had always been so formal. "How is this night for you?" he asked, finally.

"Very fine," Benito said.

"How good, how good," said Ramiro, smiling so much that he used Benito's favorite doubled words.

"Are you okay?" Benito asked.

"I am," he said.

"Are you sure? Do you need some water?"

"Yes, I do, I do really. Let me get some."

"You do not look well," Benito told him.

Benito was not trying to sell anything, but they went inside the store anyway, and Ramiro bought a big bottle and said thank you.

It was late enough when he got into his cave *departamento*. As soon as he came through, Loli heard him and was crying at the bathroom window. He flipped on one bit of light on his way to her. She was so thrilled he was there, Ramiro really did think it was as much about him. She was going wild smelling him, desperate like an addict, whimpering, both sad and happy.

"Have you been alone all day? Outside here and nobody to play with you and hold you? Poor Loli, poor poor Loli. It's hard for you to be alone, isn't it, Loli? I wish I could let you come in with me. I don't think you're dirty, and you're a good dog. You are a good dog, my Loli."

Ramiro went to the table and turned on the light and decided today he would not read about Porfirio Díaz. He was always more interested in finding new words in Spanish than in the learning itself, but this time his random page was at *Evolución* from the old encyclopedia: "... *el proceso en que todo cambia en el tiempo,* and within a species there is always variation, causing more success of some individuals within this species and less to others." It's not as if he didn't know about this concept, but the church bells were ringing. He heard someone whistling. Then came the spray and pop of fireworks. He heard a child calling out, excited. Elda? Cars out there, going and going. Like cars passing all the time, old ones to new ones. He tried to think, with scientific neutrality, of this life and death. How to take that into his own individual being, his less, his more, his here, his there, his then, his now, his next.

When the mattress moved—way too much because he slept so soundly, and deeply, for hours—Ramiro got up and pushed it back uphill. He said Loli's name and she whimpered weakly, more satisfied than tormented. He woke up again in the morning rested, full of energy, though first the aim was still for coffee. He didn't even want bread.

"Good morning," he told Benito.

Benito stood, and he was about to say good morning back when a customer came up and interrupted him and he went into his store instead.

Ramiro went to the grandmother who sold the *fruta*.

"You're early, young man!" she said. "Why are you so early?"

"Not so early."

"How are you feeling?" she asked. "Are you okay? How are you?"

"*Shai yu,*" he tried, smiling.

She laughed, shaking her head. "Ahh, where did you learn that?"

"Yesterday," he told her, "in Teotitlán del Valle."

She was still laughing. "I don't know so much."

"Aren't you Zapotec?"

"Yes, I am originally from Coyotepec, but my family didn't teach me our language. I know words."

"*Bwen,*" he said.

She laughed again. "*Bhel,*" she told him, pointing to what seemed like the peanuts. "That is meat. And *ghen,* that is chile." She gave him a small bag of the nuts. "You eat."

"*Ghen,*" he said. "I already can't remember the other!"

"*Bhel.*"

"*Bhel,*" he said. "And now I forgot what chile is!"

"*Ghen.*" She laughed. "*Ghet,* that is tortilla."

"Stop, teacher! I can't!"

"I can give you more," she told him, "and I don't have tortillas here."

"More than you think, I think. With the words for meat, chile, and tortilla, what more do I need?"

"Meat, chile, and tortilla." She looked carefully at Ramiro. "Are you okay, young man?"

Suddenly others arrived to buy and so he took two boxes, *piña* and *sandia*. She pulled out a plastic bag and gave him another of *coco con chile y limón* and also three cakes, shaped like *pan dulce* where he grew up, but smaller and harder. They were all she had. She looked up, smiling like a close friend, an answer to her own question to him. "You eat."

He decided to skip coffee altogether. He walked back to the *departamento*. Benito wasn't outside Abarrotes, his chair empty. Sra. Campos's car was gone, too. He bent his head through the archway after opening the wrought-iron gate, and he sat down at the table. He picked at the boxes of the fruit but he couldn't eat even one. The *pan dulce,* yellow inside, was full of sweet black seeds. After a couple of bites, he went to the bathroom window, where Loli came, and he gave her the rest.

His decision seemed sudden but wasn't. It was there the moment he walked in that first day, even if he put down his bags, intending to stay to the end. He wrote a note to Sra. Campos saying that he was sorry, but as she knew, when he stood up, he didn't fit—he kept scraping his knuckles, and it was so hard to shower, and there was the sliding bed—and so he had to leave, and he thanked her for renting to him and for the beautiful time he spent in her house. He took only a few things he brought with him, though, only enough for a day bag. He guessed that she would be mad, or upset, and he didn't wish that for her. It was how she was. She would have to learn how to accept it, and surely she would. She had so much still, and whatever bad toward him she felt, it would pass. Would it be better for her if he stayed? Or worse? Maybe it wouldn't matter either way. It could turn out exactly the same as it was now no matter when he left, how, or if he didn't walk away at all. She might complain about him, him leaving these things of his, too, until maybe, with all that was good around her—her child, Elda, even Loli—she wouldn't remember he'd ever been there.

Benito rose from his chair. "How are you?" he asked.

"Fine, fine," Ramiro told him. Saying it double made him truly happy.

"Are you okay?" Benito said in his formal manner, suspicious of Ramiro's smiling to himself.

"I'm leaving the señora's place."

"How good, how good."

"I left her a note, but will you tell her I am sorry?"

"Yes, of course."

"Tell her I said thank you."

"Surely."

They walked together to the corner of Tinoco y Palacios, the busy street that many cabs traveled.

"How good, Ramiro," Benito said. "This is right for you. It is a tomb in there."

He shook Benito's hand.

"Where will you go?" he asked Ramiro.

A taxi stopped. Ramiro shook his hand good-bye yet again, said, "Thank you so much," got in, and Benito walked slowly back to the chair outside his store.